ANDROMEDA STORIES

VOLUME I

KEIKO TAKEMIYA

STORY BY RYU MITSUSE

VERTICAL.

Translation—Magnolia Steele
Production—Hiroko Mizuno
Shinobu Sato
Ayako Fukumitsu
Akane Ishida
Mami Yamada

Published by Vertical, Inc., New York.

Originally serialized in Japanese as *Andoromeda Storizu*
in *Gekkan Manga Shonen* and *Gekkan Manga Duo* (later *Duo*),
Asahi Sonorama, 1980-82.

ISBN 1-932234-84-5 / 978-1-932234-84-8

Manufactured in the United States of America

First Edition

Vertical, Inc.
1185 Avenue of the Americas, 32nd Floor
New York, NY, 10036
www.vertical-inc.com

ANDROMEDA STORIES

TEN BILLION... NO

FIFTY BILLION, OR WAS IT A HUNDRED BILLION YEARS AGO?

BEFORE THE CREATION OF THE UNIVERSE...

IT WAS A BALL OF ENERGY TWELVE BILLION KILOMETERS IN DIAMETER.

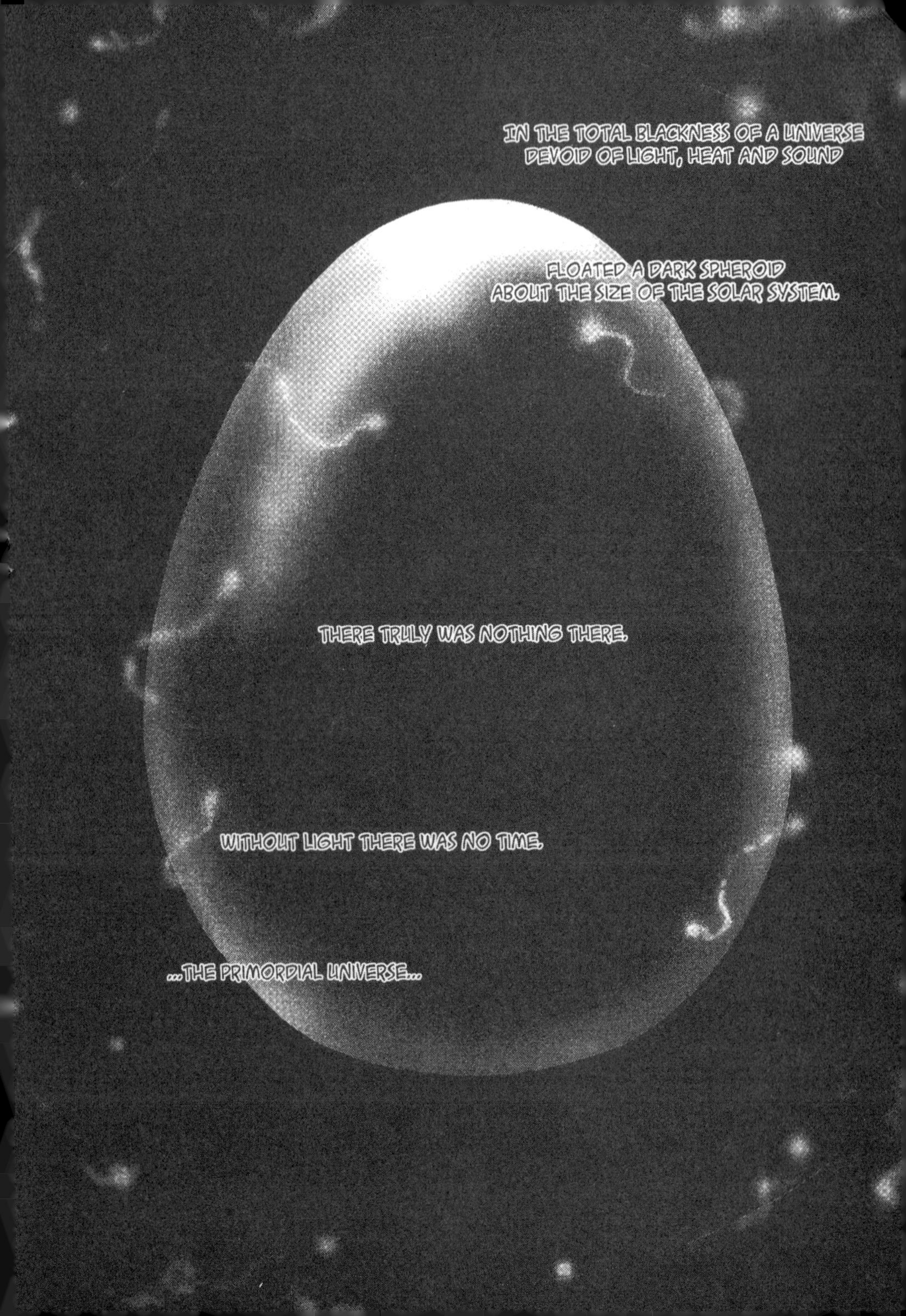

IN THE TOTAL BLACKNESS OF A UNIVERSE
DEVOID OF LIGHT, HEAT AND SOUND

FLOATED A DARK SPHEROID
ABOUT THE SIZE OF THE SOLAR SYSTEM.

THERE TRULY WAS NOTHING THERE.

WITHOUT LIGHT THERE WAS NO TIME.

...THE PRIMORDIAL UNIVERSE...

YET

TIME FLOWED WHERE THERE WAS NO TIME;
AN ETERNITY PASSED WHERE THERE WAS NO HOUR.

AND THEN—ONCE UPON THAT TIME

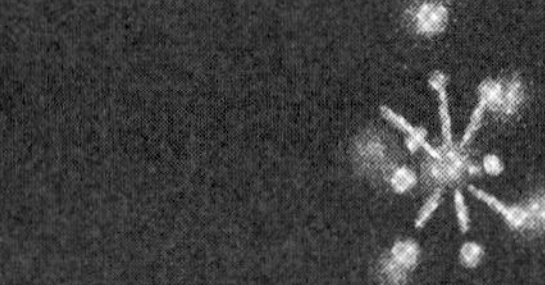

THE BALL OF ENERGY
SUDDENLY BEGAN TO TURN INTO MATTER,
THE BITS OF MATTER, AT FIRST SPREAD OUT OVER MIND-BOGGLING DISTANCES,
MATTER AKIN TO NEUTRON.
NOW AT THE END OF ETERNITY
DRIFTED TOGETHER AT LAST
TO FORM A THIN NEUTRONIC CLOUD,
TUGGING AT ONE ANOTHER BY FORCE OF GRAVITY,
INCREASING IN DENSITY.

THE DENSE MATTER GENERATED HEAT

INTERACTED FURTHER,

AND AMIDST
THE EXTREME DENSITY
AND TEMPERATURE

ULTIMATELY

EXPLODING IN A BIG BANG—

THUS
"SPACE" AND "TIME" WERE BORN.

FROM PAST TOWARDS FUTURE
THE COSMOS EXPANDED,

TIME FLOWING AT THE SPEED
AT WHICH IT EXPANDED.

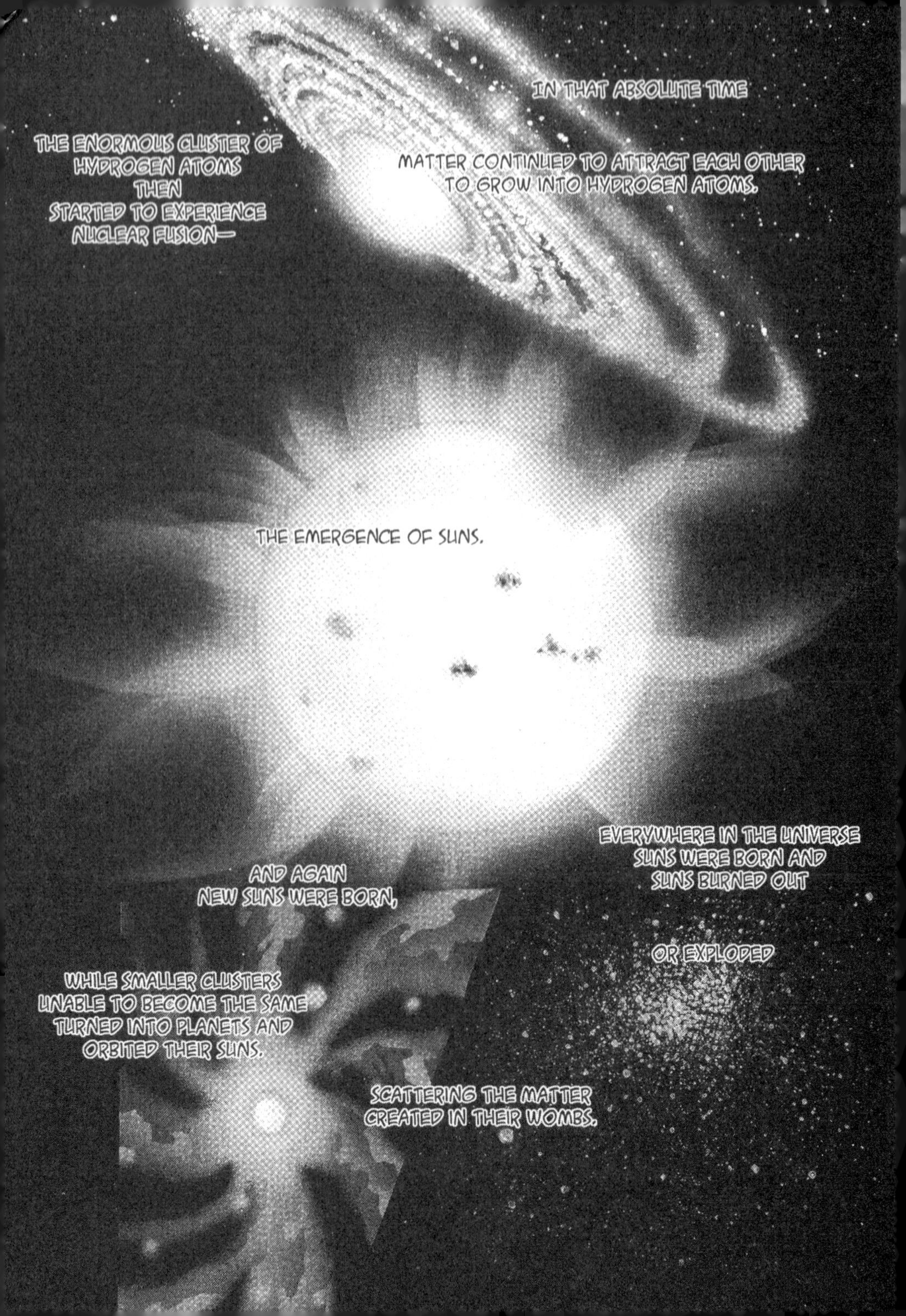

IN THAT ABSOLUTE TIME

MATTER CONTINUED TO ATTRACT EACH OTHER
TO GROW INTO HYDROGEN ATOMS.

THE ENORMOUS CLUSTER OF
HYDROGEN ATOMS
THEN
STARTED TO EXPERIENCE
NUCLEAR FUSION—

THE EMERGENCE OF SUNS.

EVERYWHERE IN THE UNIVERSE
SUNS WERE BORN AND
SUNS BURNED OUT

OR EXPLODED

SCATTERING THE MATTER
CREATED IN THEIR WOMBS.

AND AGAIN
NEW SUNS WERE BORN,

WHILE SMALLER CLUSTERS
UNABLE TO BECOME THE SAME
TURNED INTO PLANETS AND
ORBITED THEIR SUNS.

THE FLOW OF A HUNDRED BILLION YEARS—

THE SCATTERED CLOUDS OF HYDROGEN WAFTING IN THE VAST UNIVERSE

THUS SEPARATELY DREW AND SPUN TOGETHER,

GROWING INTO NEBULAE.

THE DISTANCE TO ONE OF THOSE NEBULAE, THE ANDROMEDA GALAXY, IS 2.2 MILLION LIGHT-YEARS;

THE ANDROMEDA GALAXY WE SEE UP IN THE SKY TONIGHT IS THE ONE THAT EXISTED 2.2 MILLION LONG YEARS AGO,

WHEN NO RECOGNIZABLE ANCESTOR OF MANKIND HAD YET APPEARED ON EARTH.

A FAINT STAIN OF LIGHT
THAT FLOATS IN THE NIGHT SKY,
ANDROMEDA
STIRS STRANGE ROMANCES
IN THOSE WHO BEHOLD IT.

LOOK, MOM,
THERE GOES A HERD OF SAND DRAGONS.
THEY'RE LIKELY HEADED FOR THE WATER HOLE.

I SHOULD GO WITH THEM AND BRING BACK WATER.
IT'LL SOON BE NIGHT.

TAKE CARE.
YOU TOO, MOM!
JIMSA...
DOES THE BOY UNDERSTAND?
IT'S BEEN FIVE CYCLES SINCE WE BEGAN LIVING IN THE BADLANDS.

PLANET ASTRIAS
THE COSMORALIAN EMPIRE

THE MONTH WHEN BLUE PISCES IS CROSSED BY A WHITE RAINBOW

FIFTH DAY—

AND

ANKLETS, ARMLETS, AND BRACELETS ...

BRACELETS ENGRAVED, MILORD, WITH THE LUCKY NUMBER 8.

AH!

WASN'T THIS A GIFT FROM HIS ROYAL HIGHNESS ITHACA? WHAT A GORGEOUS NECKLACE!

A TIARA, TASSELS, AND A COIN CROWN, AND—
ENOUGH, NURSE TARAMA!
IT MAKES ME SICK JUST TO SEE THEM LAID OUT,
BUT YOUR ITEMIZING THEM IS GIVING ME STIFF SHOULDERS.
THINK OF LILIA WHO'D ACTUALLY HAVE TO WEAR ALL THAT JEWELRY!
IT'D BREAK HER NECK!
S-SUCH BLASPHEMY!
WHAT DO YOU TAKE THIS FOR?
A BRIDE IS MOST SUSCEPTIBLE TO EVIL FORCES! ARE YOU SAYING WE SHOULD SEND OUR PRINCESS OFF WITHOUT CHARMS?

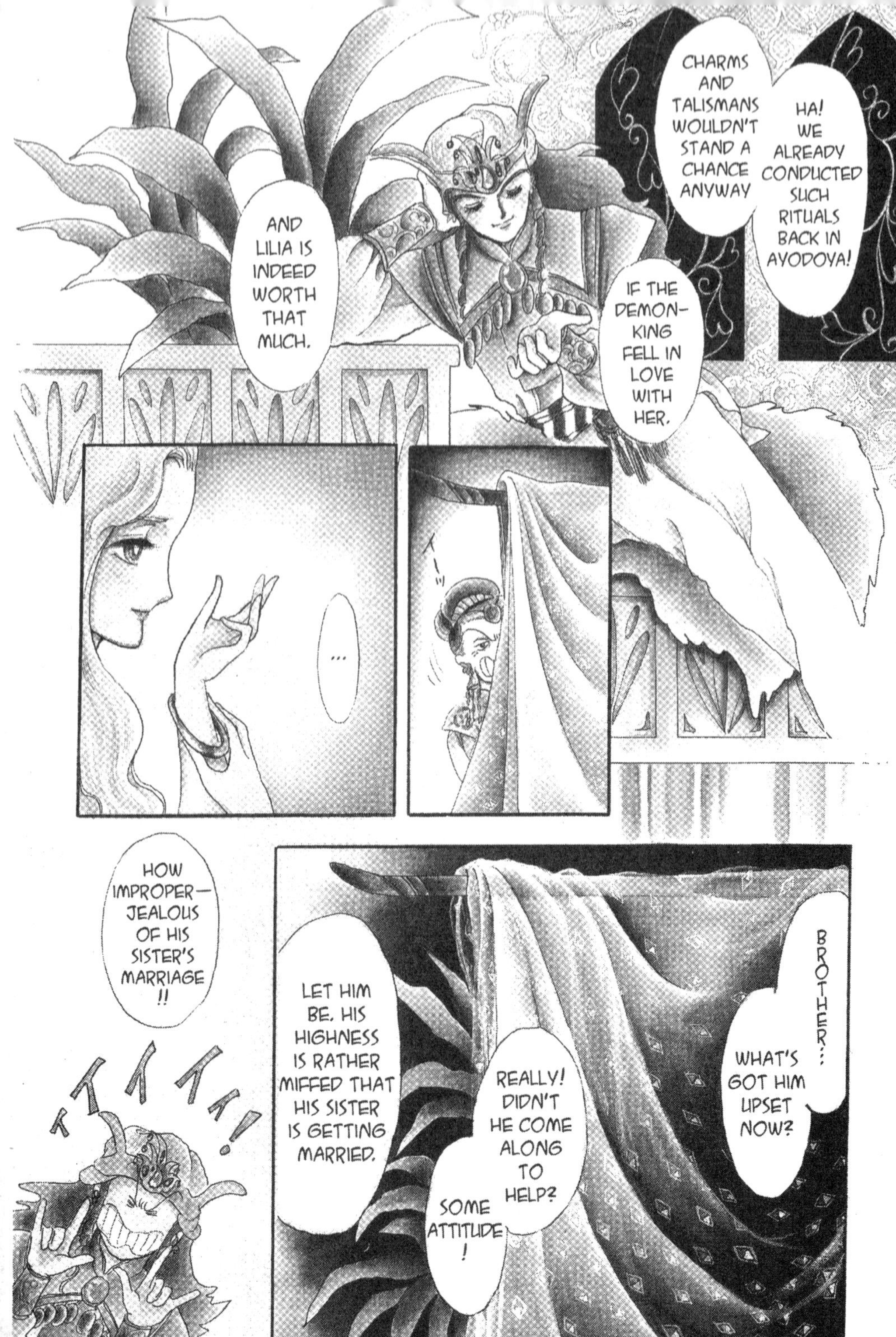
HA! WE ALREADY CONDUCTED SUCH RITUALS BACK IN AYODOYA!
CHARMS AND TALISMANS WOULDN'T STAND A CHANCE ANYWAY
IF THE DEMON-KING FELL IN LOVE WITH HER.
AND LILIA IS INDEED WORTH THAT MUCH.
...
BROTHER...
WHAT'S GOT HIM UPSET NOW?
REALLY! DIDN'T HE COME ALONG TO HELP?
SOME ATTITUDE!
LET HIM BE. HIS HIGHNESS IS RATHER MIFFED THAT HIS SISTER IS GETTING MARRIED.
HOW IMPROPER—JEALOUS OF HIS SISTER'S MARRIAGE!!

NOW... HAVE A LOOK, PRINCE MILAN.
AYODOYA'S PRINCESS, THE PEERLESS BEAUTY, RESPLENDENT IN HER MOMENT OF GLORY!

LILIA...
BROTHER...
WHAT'S THE MATTER,
CAT GOT YOUR TONGUE?
THAT'S NOT IT... I'M CONFUSED. I WANT TO EMBRACE HER...
BASTARD! EVEN IF ITHACA IS MY FRIEND I WANT TO KILL HIM!
WHAT A THING TO SAY TO YOUR SISTER ON HER WEDDING DAY!
ENOUGH OF YOUR JESTS, MAY THE DEVIL FEAST ON YOU!
But I was serious...

ARANCHAN,
CAPITAL OF COSMORALIA
ポン！
ポポン
ワー

ARTEIL CASTLE
ワァ
ワァ
ワァ
ワイ
ワイ

WHAT TIME DOES IT BEGIN?
NOON!
HEY, THAT'S MY SPOT!
ワイ ワイ
TOO MANY HANGING BASKETS! THE TREE'S GONNA BREAK. IT'S BREAKING!!
ARGH, NO!

WELL, WELL...
SOME COM-MOTION THIS IS.
WHAT'S IT ALL ABOUT?

UH

I'M A THREAD BUYER. I ARRIVED HERE FROM THE WEST EARLY THIS MORNING.
WHY SHOULD I?
HUH?
YOU MEAN YOU DON'T KNOW?

THAT ISN'T ALL. HE'S ALSO TAKING A BRIDE AT THE CORONATION.
THEN A WEDDING TOO!

HOW ABOUT THAT! THOUGH I DID KNOW THE CROWN PRINCE WAS ASSUMING THE THRONE...

YOU'RE IN LUCK, MY OLD MAN! THE NEW KING IS BEING CROWNED TODAY.
A HAPPY DAY THAT DOESN'T COME OFTEN IN ONE'S LIFETIME!

THAT'LL MAKE A GREAT STORY, BUT WON'T THE CORONATION BE HELD IN THE PALACE?
GATHERING HERE DOESN'T MEAN YOU'LL SEE ANY OF IT...
BUT WE WILL!
AFTER THE WEDDING, THE KING AND QUEEN ARE COMING OUT ON THE BALCONY
TO GREET US ALL!
WE'LL ALSO GET TO SEE THE MINISTERS AND GENERALS ARRIVING FOR THE CELEBRATION.
LOOKS LIKE THEY'VE COME WHILE WE WERE CHAT-TING.
WHO'S FIRST?
CARE TO BET?
AH!
THE MINIS-TERS ARE HERE!
DON'T PUSH.

HIS EXCEL-LENCY PRIME MINISTER BUHO!

ギ キ
HIS EXCELLENCY BUHO?
HE'S THE NEW KING'S— CROWN PRINCE ITHACA'S— UNCLE.
AN ELDER BROTHER OF THE OLD KING.
HE LET HIS BROTHER BE KING AND SETTLED FOR PREMIER?
AND CONTROLLED POLITICS. A SHREWD MAN MORE POWERFUL THAN THE KING.
IT'S THE DRAGON CAVALRY!
WOW, COOL!
ザッ
ザッ
ザッ
ザッ

IT'S GEN-ERAL VALT!
PRETTY STATELY TO BRING OUT THE DRAGON CAVALRY.
ME, I DON'T LIKE HIM.
HE'S AN ARROGANT SCHEMER.
LOOK! THE DUKE OF EAGLE,
HIS WIFE AS PRETTY AS EVER!
THERE'S GRAND DUKE BRIK AND HIS DAUGH-TER.
WOW WOW WOW!

のそり
GUESS I SHOULD GET GOING TOO!
SIR BALGA!
IT'S SIR BALGA THE SWORDS-MAN!
YOU WERE RIGHT HERE ALL THIS TIME ?!
HIS EASYGOING CHARM KILLS ME!
SALUTE!

ON BEHALF OF THE KING OF AYODOYA,
HIS ROYAL HIGHNESS PRINCE MILAN!
THAT RED HAIR RUNS IN AYODOYA'S HEIRS.
HE'S LOVELY...
HE'S SO SLIM!
HE'S THE ELDER BROTHER OF THE PRINCESS BRIDE.
I ENVY HER!
HE'S MORE HANDSOME THAN OUR CROWN PRINCE ITHACA
OH, YOU TRAITOR!

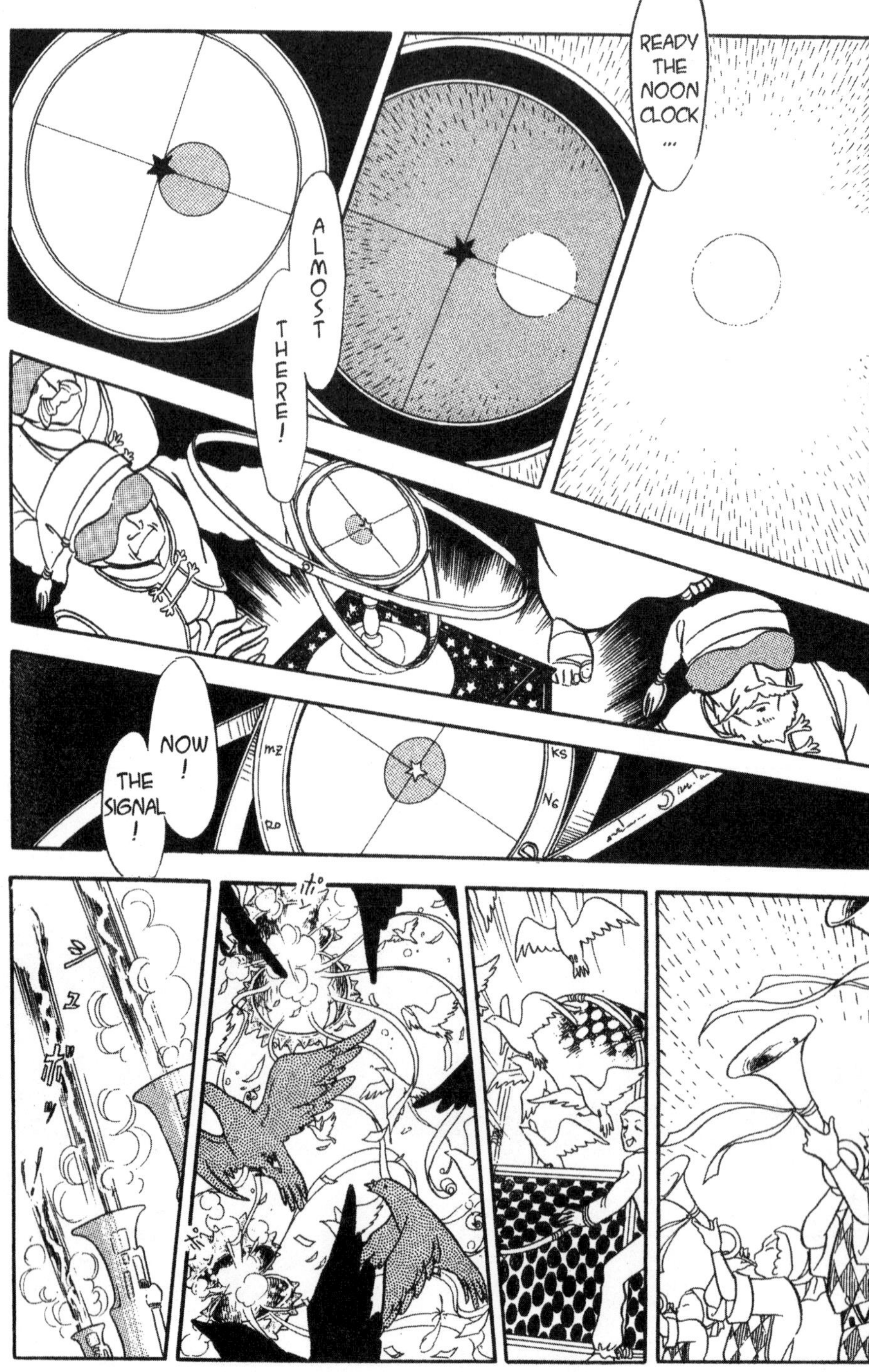
READY THE NOON CLOCK ...
ALMOST THERE!
NOW!
THE SIGNAL!

THE CORONATION BEGINS!
LOOK!

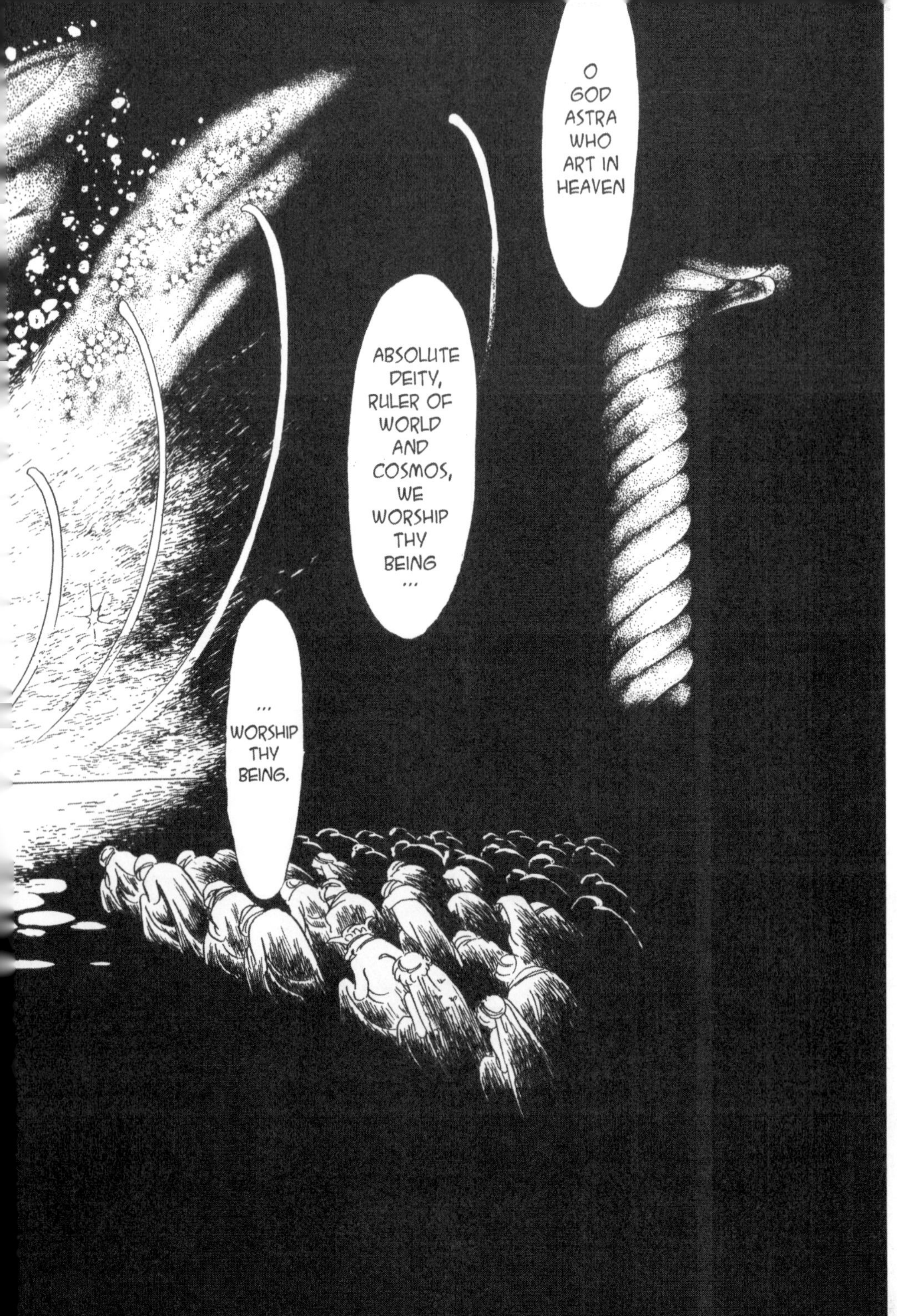
O GOD ASTRA WHO ART IN HEAVEN
ABSOLUTE DEITY, RULER OF WORLD AND COSMOS, WE WORSHIP THY BEING ...
... WORSHIP THY BEING.

OUR HOLY LORD SWEARS TO TRUST THY WILL AND ABIDE BY IT TO LEAD HIS PEOPLE AND RULE THEM WISELY.

HIS ROYAL HIGHNESS CROWN PRINCE ITHACA'S CORONATION CEREMONY SHALL NOW BEGIN.
ANY OPPOSED TO THIS, SPEAK UP.
OPPOSED? LET THE MAN COME FORTH! I'LL KILL HIM MYSELF!
TO DARE OPPOSE THE AUGUST CORONATION OF HIS MAJESTY ASTRALTA III!
STEADY, GENERAL... HE'S JUST FOLLOWING CUSTOM.
CROWN PRINCE,
PLEASE STEP FOR-WARD.

SO THE TIME HAS COME, ITHACA.
YOU'LL BE KING OF A REALM, SOMEONE THAT I'LL NEED TO ADDRESS FORMALLY.

CROWN PRINCE ITHACA,
DO YOU SWEAR TO REVERE THE GOD ASTRA AND ABIDE BY HIS WILL TO RULE WISELY?
I DO.

YEAR ZERO OF THE PAPACY—AT THIS MOMENT, CROWN PRINCE ITHACA BECAME ASTRALTA II.

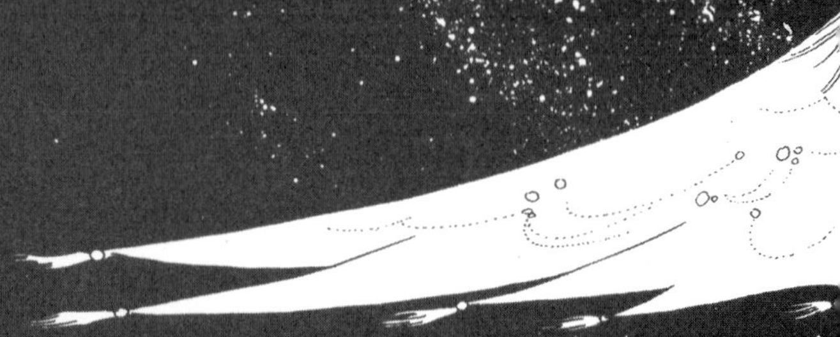
FROM THE POSITIONS OF THE STARS TO THE BRIGHTNESS OF THE SUN, IT WAS SUPPOSED TO BE THE PERFECT DAY.
THE MONTH WHEN BLUE PISCES IS CROSSED BY A WHITE RAINBOW. FIFTH DAY.

THAT A SMALL, ILL-BODING STAR HAD SLIPPED INTO THE CELESTIAL CONFIGURATION

AND WAS BEING DRAWN TOWARDS PLANET ASTRIAS,

NONE DID NOTICE.

MK1 PAPACY YEAR 0

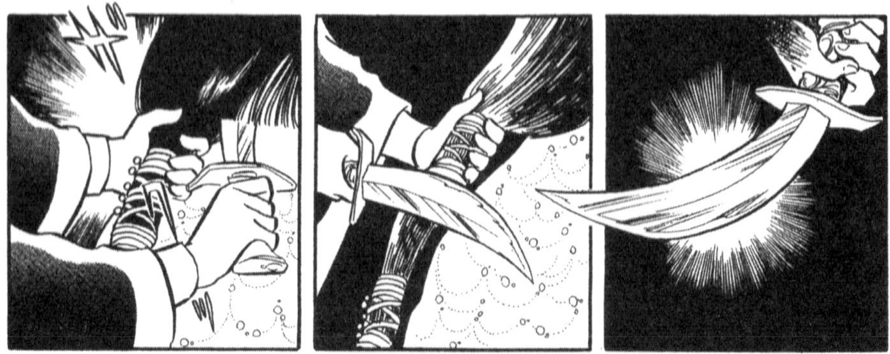

THE KING HAS PLEDGED HIS SOUL TO GOD.
... TO GOD.
THE PROOF!

AMAMEDAYANA YANAYANAMEDA AMAMEDAYANA
KING, TAKE THE THRONE.
ASTRA KANAM ASTRA SARSUL
AMAMEDAYANA YANAYANAMEDA
KING, TAKE THE THRONE.
KING, TAKE THE THRONE!!
オー オー
オー オー

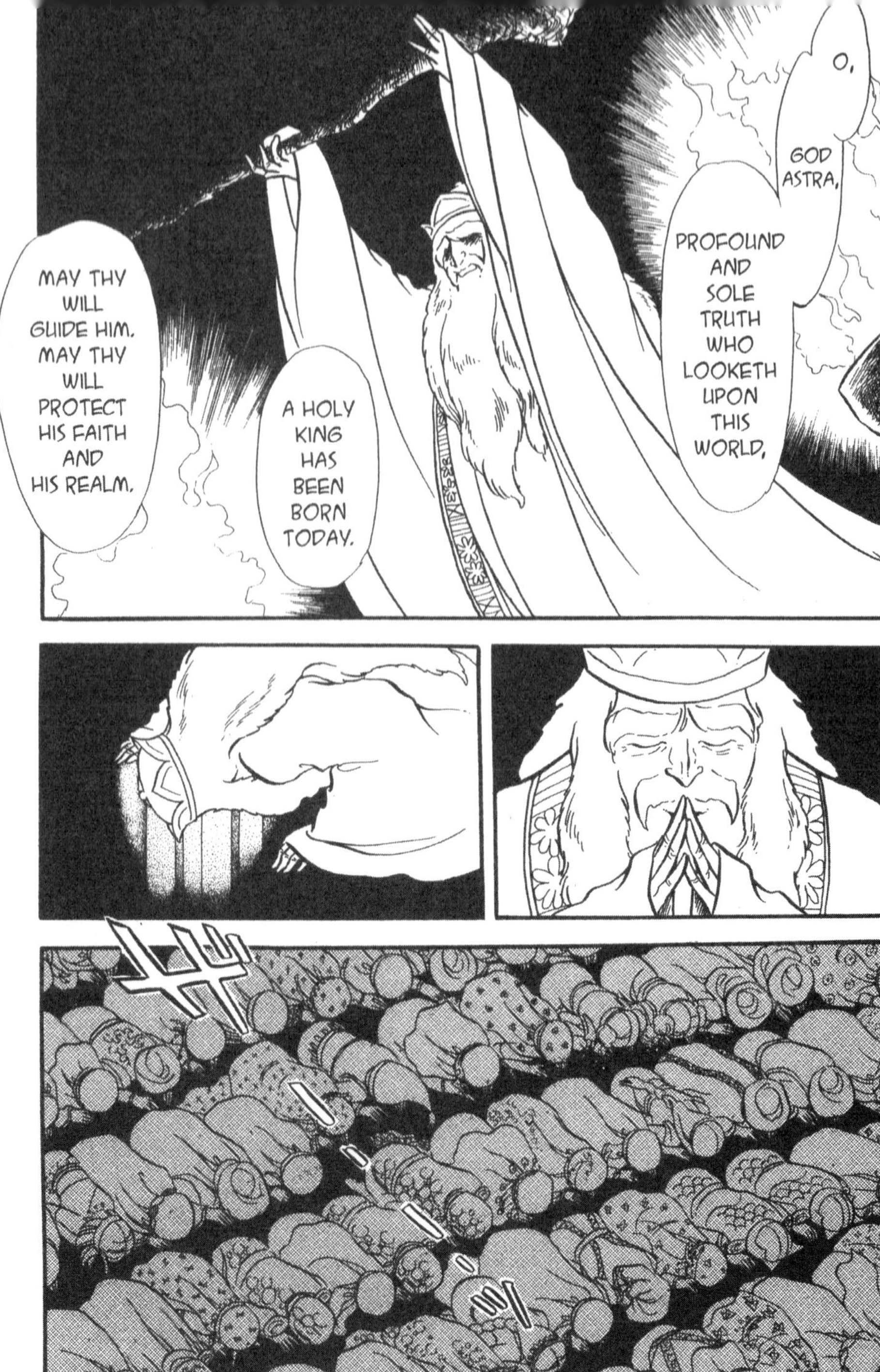
O,
GOD ASTRA,
PROFOUND AND SOLE TRUTH WHO LOOKETH UPON THIS WORLD,
A HOLY KING HAS BEEN BORN TODAY.
MAY THY WILL GUIDE HIM. MAY THY WILL PROTECT HIS FAITH AND HIS REALM.

WE WILL PROCEED TO THE NEW KING ASTRALTA III'S WEDDING.
WILL HIS BETROTHED PRINCESS LILIA ENTER.
おおお…
...HOW BEAUTIFUL!
TRULY THE GREAT-EST BEAUTY OF AYO-DOYA...
FROM NOW COSMO-RALIA'S,
NAY, ASTRIA'S GREATEST BEAUTY!
PRIN-CESS LILIA!

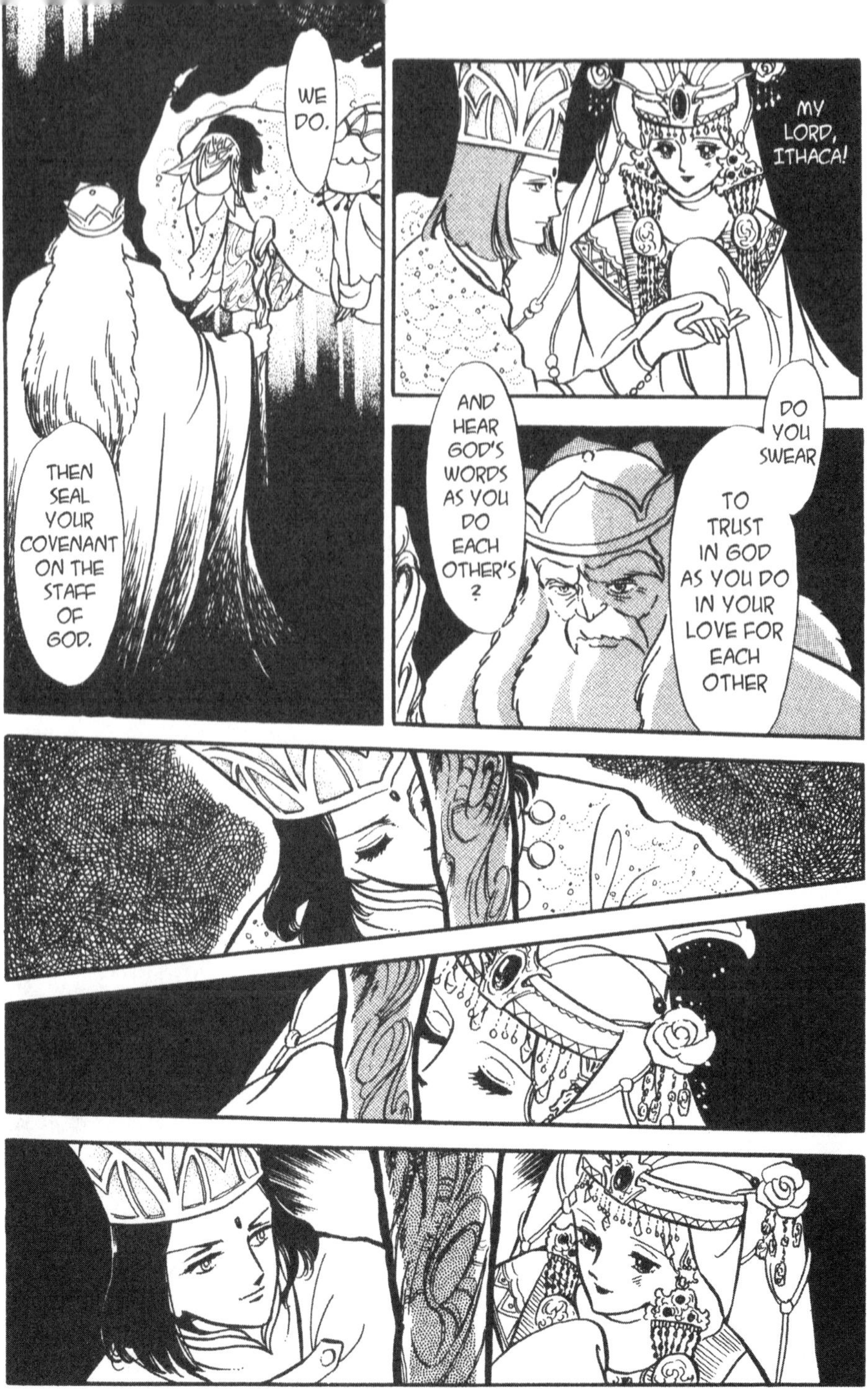

DO YOU SWEAR TO TRUST IN GOD AS YOU DO IN YOUR LOVE FOR EACH OTHER

AND HEAR GOD'S WORDS AS YOU DO EACH OTHER'S?

WE DO.

THEN SEAL YOUR COVENANT ON THE STAFF OF GOD.

MY LORD, ITHACA!

ワー
ワー
ワー
ワー
ワー

LONG LIVE THE NEW KING!
LONG LIVE THE QUEEN!
A FEAST! THE CASTLE OPENS ITS GATES!
EAT AND DRINK ALL YOU CAN!
SING!
DANCE!

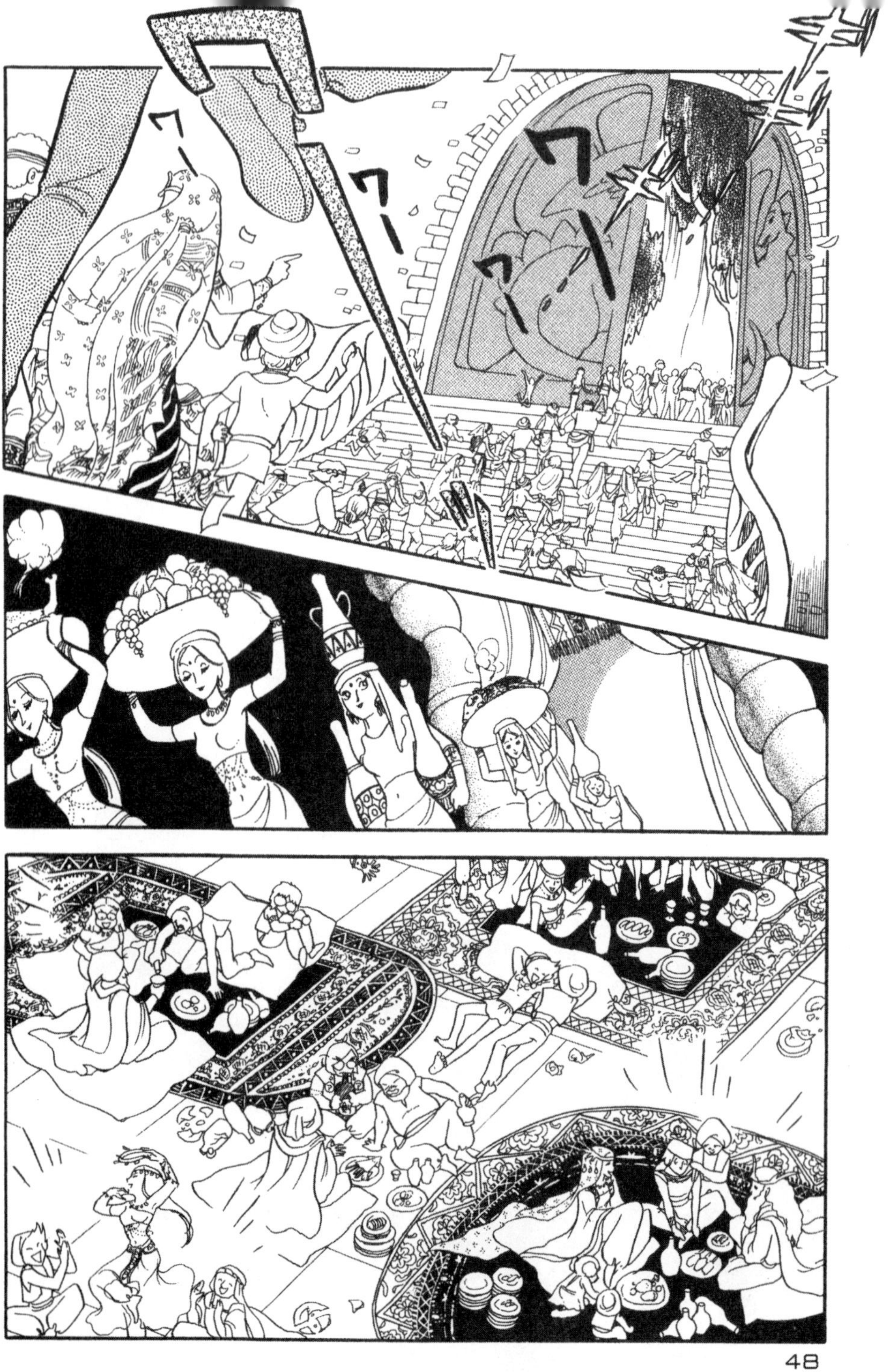

ワー
ワー
ワー
ワー

EATING CONTEST

SUCH A PEACEFUL COUNTRY!
IS THIS HALCYON REALM TO FALL TO RUINS, TOO— LIKE RODLIAN?
I DON'T WANT TO BELIEVE IT.
I DON'T WANT TO, BUT...
MOVE!
LOOK OUT!
HICC
SORRY ABOUT THAT, DEAR GUEST!
HA!
HAHAHA...
NOW, WHO'S NEXT? THERE'S 1,000 CREDITS IN IT FOR ANYONE WHO CAN BEAT ME!
ワア
ワァ ワァ

のっし!
ARR
I'LL FIGHT YOU, GLADIATOR BALGA.
IF I WIN, I'LL HAVE SOMETHING TO BOAST OF BACK HOME
AND THE 1,000 CREDITS, TOO.
I'M GODEM OF THE CHAIN, FROM BETHLA IN THE WEST.
ジリ…
YOUR INTRO CAN WAIT 'TIL AFTER YOU WIN,
BALDIE!
COME GET ME!
DON'T BE CRYING WHEN YOU GET THIS IN YOUR CHEEK.
SIR BALGA, DON'T DO THIS!

WHOA

WHAT'S THE MATTER? YOU SOUNDED BOLD!
NONE OF YOU CAN EVEN MAKE ME DRAW MY SWORD? COWARDS!
ヒック
…クス
YOU THERE ...!
DID YOU JUST LAUGH?
HEAVENS, NO, MIGHTY GLADIATOR,
WHY WOULD I LAUGH?
YOUR SKILL TOOK MY BREATH AWAY.

I HEARD YOU LAUGH, AND WHO LAUGHS IN AWE?
YOU APPEAR TO BE A MERE LAD,
BUT YOUR YOUTH IS NO EXCUSE TO ME.
I'LL TEACH YOU TO RESPECT YOUR ELDERS.
DON'T DARE WALK AWAY!
YOU THINK I'M BLIND?
I SEE A SWORD UNDER THAT THIN SILK OF YOURS!
アレー

HIS BEARING IS NO ORDINARY LAD'S.
THE CASTLE'S BEEN THROWN OPEN FOR THE HAPPY DAY.
IF THERE'S TROUBLE, IT'S TO A MILITARY AIDE'S SHAME!
I MAY BE DRUNK, BUT I HAVEN'T FORGOTTEN MY ROLE.
AARGH
ON WITH IT AND FACE ME!

YOU ARE HOPE-LESS. CAN'T YOU SEE...
I'M NO SHADY CHAR-ACTER?
チッ
A...
PRETTY!
WO
WOM-AN
WO
SHUDDUP!
ぷるぷる
I'LL KNOW IF YOU'RE SUSPECT WHEN OUR SWORDS MEET!
TRUE
THEY SAY THE SWORD TELLS THE PERSON.
HMM
...A PERFECT GUARD!

YAA

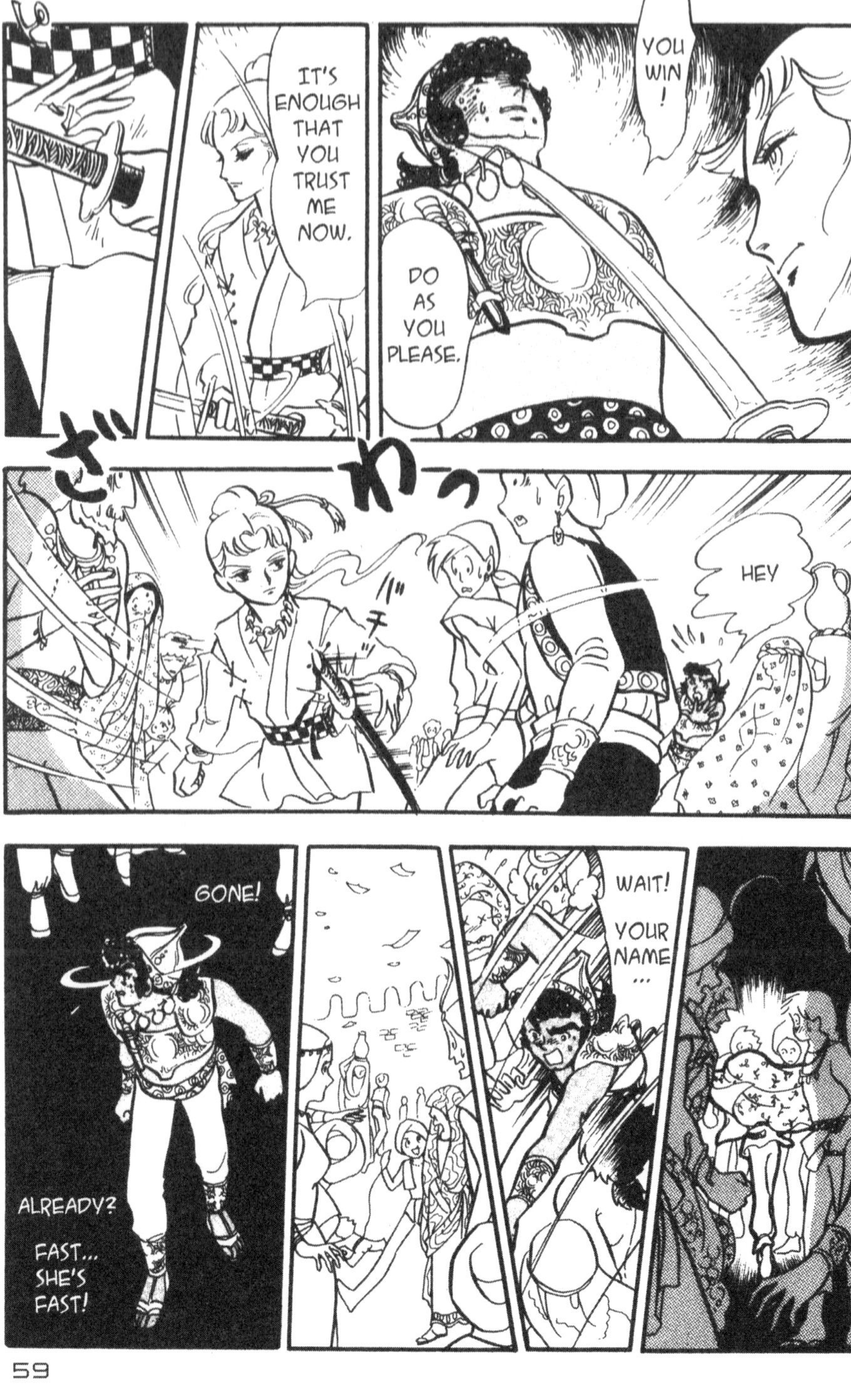

YOU WIN!
DO AS YOU PLEASE.
IT'S ENOUGH THAT YOU TRUST ME NOW.
ざわっ
HEY
バチ

A DRINK, MY LORD.

LILIA...
YOU MUST BE TIRED, TAKE YOUR REST.
NO, I'D RATHER BE BY YOUR SIDE.

MY, ALREADY SO MANY STARS!
ASTRA GOD'S STARS... LILIA, I SWEAR, AGAIN, ON THOSE STARS:
PEACE FOR THIS REALM, AND HAPPINESS
FOR YOU.
MY LORD!
I HEARD YOU WERE GOOD AT ASTROMETRY.
THAT EXCEPTIONALLY BRIGHT STAR— WHAT IS ITS NAME?
IN THE BLUE PISCES CONSTELLATION? HMM...

STRANGE... THERE NEVER WAS SUCH A STAR IN IT.
A NEW STAR...? I'LL HAVE THEM LOOK INTO IT.
PERHAPS YOU BROUGHT WITH YOU THE STAR OF A BEAUTIFUL DESTINY.
IT SHINES AS BRIGHTLY AS YOU DO.
IF IT HAS NO NAME YET
I SHALL NAME IT
LILIA...
WHO WOULD HAVE THOUGHT IT AN ILL-FATED STAR?
AS THE FESTIVE NIGHT DEEPENED, EVER LUMINOUS SHONE THE STAR.

BLUE PISCES 45
BLUE PISCES 57
BLUE PISCES 64
THEN WE'LL LEVY NO TAXES ON FARMERS IN THE EIN OU SÉLAT RIVER DISTRICT
UNTIL THE RIVER'S LEVEE WORK IS COMPLETE.
ARE WE AGREED?
GOOD, LET US ADJOURN.
ガタ
ガタン
THE KING RETIRES!

WHAT A COMPAS-SIONATE KING! THE EIN OU SÉLAT FARMERS WILL BE JUBILANT.
AS PUBLIC WELFARE MINISTER, I'M GLAD TOO.

FAR TOO SOFT.
HE'S STILL GREEN. NO TAXES AT ALL!

NOT MUCH WE CAN DO, IT'S THE KING'S OWN RULING.
TSK!

AT LEAST WE'LL EARN POINTS WITH THE MASSES.
AS LONG AS WE SQUEEZE THEM ELSEWHERE ...
STILL ...!

USED
COME AND GET IT!
10 BIRDS FOR 20 RADISHES. IT'S A STEAL !

HOW ABOUT A USED DINOSAUR?
IT'S TAME, WORKED AS LIVESTOCK FOR 50 YEARS. MILD-TEMPERED, SIMPLE DIET, FERTILE.
THIS ONE HAS 102 YEARS, BUT IT'LL LIVE ANOTHER 100.
1,000 CREDITS, NO MORE.
STURDY BODY, PERFECT FOR PLASTERING AND DIGGING.
WILL IT SERVE AS A STEP STOOL?
OUCH
NO, SIR! SLIMY MOCK-SNAPPERS HAVE SLIPPERY SKIN.
パク
YOWZA
HE BIT ME! HE BIT ME!

UH-OH!
ONCE HE BITES, HE WON'T LET GO 'TIL IT THUNDERS.
OW OW OW, DO SOMETHING!
めっ
THUNDER, DID YOU SAY? HOW ABOUT THIS?
BAA
SAY, LET ME ASK YOU,
HAVE YOU SEEN A SWORDS-WOMAN?
WOMAN? DOESN'T COME TO MIND
IS SHE YOUR SQUEEZE, BOSS?
IDIOT!!
I'M ONLY CHECKING UP ON HER
BECAUSE SHE'S NOT FROM AROUND HERE!

Dude's loud.
PEACE IS MAKING YOU ALL WAY TOO LAX!
THANK YOU. THANK YOU, SIR.

WELL DONE.
IT'S ALL WE GET THESE DAYS.
THE DRAGON CAVALRY FINDS IT A BORE.
HAIL GENERAL VALT!
LONG LIVE
THE DRAGON CAVALRY!
NAP
SHH
MOM, MAY I FREE THE BIRDS WE GOT IN TOWN?
YES, DO.
BIRDS LIKE THE SKY BEST AND FISH LIKE THE RIVER BEST.
IN THE FOREST, MAN AND BEAST LIVE HAPPILY TOGETHER.

ピチュピチュ
DAD, THERE ARE DEER IN THE GARDEN!
GIVE THEM SOME BREAD.
IT'S ALL WE'VE LEFT FOR TODAY, BUT ALL CREATURES DESERVE THEIR BLESSING.
ピィチチチチチ…
WAIT IN LINE. THE OLD MAN OF THE FOREST IS BUSY.
MY HUSBAND FELL FROM THE ROOF AND HURT HIS BACK!
HE'LL HEAL IN NO TIME.
MY SON WAS CRUSHED BY A STONE WALL LAST MONTH AND THE OLD MAN OF THE FOREST BROUGHT HIM BACK TO LIFE!
あああん!
THERE, THERE. ALMOST DONE.
プチ
ピタッ
YOUR CHEST DOESN'T HURT NOW, DOES IT?
A LITTLE MEDICINE, AND YOU'LL BE GOOD AS NEW.

LOOK! HE'S ALL FINE!
HE HAD A HIGH FEVER AND WAS CRYING SINCE LAST NIGHT...
THANK YOU, THANK YOU SO MUCH!
WORK'S BEEN SPARSE, I'VE VERY LITTLE MONEY.
I DO HAVE THESE ...
NO, KEEP YOUR MONEY. I'LL JUST TAKE THOSE.
THEY MAKE GOOD STOMACH MEDICINE.
HM?
HELP US, OLD MASTER!
A WORKER AT THE STEEL PLANT GOT MOLTEN STEEL ON HIM...
LAY HIM DOWN THERE!
IF THAT'S ALL, I CAN HEAL HIM.

ザワ
ザワ
ザワ
HE'S A GONER. HE WAS BURNT TO TOAST!
EVEN THE OLD MAN CAN'T SAVE THAT ONE ...
OKAY, THIS... AND THIS...
AND THIS. MIX THEM WELL! IT'S GOING IN THE NEBULIZER.
MOCA

ワッ!
THANK YOU.
TAKE CARE. CHANGE YOUR BANDAGES ONCE A DAY.
WOW! MAGIC...
IT'S PROPER MEDI-CINE.
I BET YOU'RE THE ONLY DOCTOR OF YOUR KIND!
ザワザワ
HMM, A STRANGE WIND BLOWS...
AH, YOU SENSE IT TOO? THERE, THERE.
I HOPE IT'S NOT AN ILL OMEN...

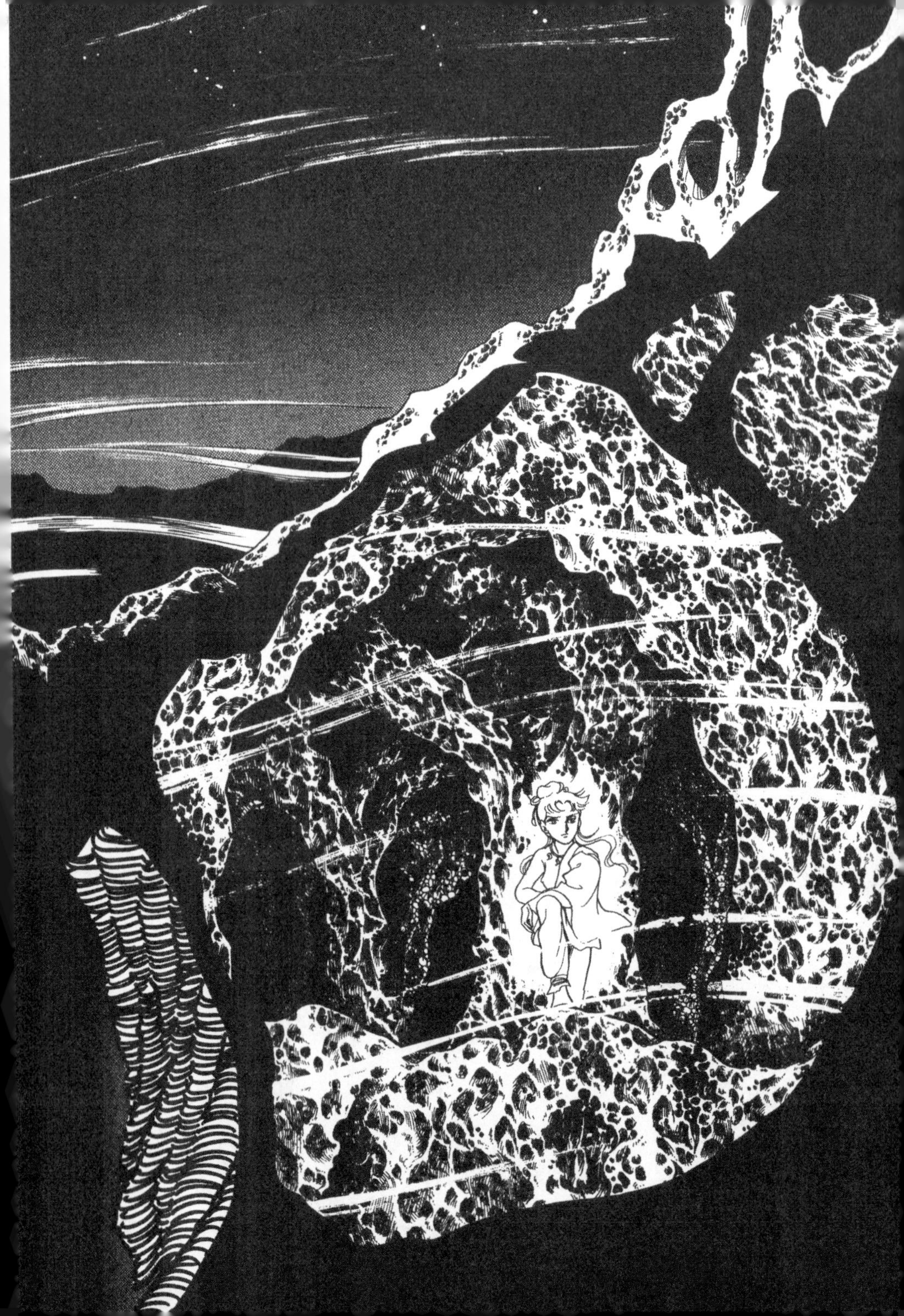

THE WIND...
I HAVE A BAD FEELING.
A PREMONITION?
IF SO, IT'S IMMINENT.

UH-UH.
THIS ISN'T A PSYCHOLOGICAL ATTACK.
TO BE RECALLING RODLIAN...
I MUST BE TIRED

IN THAT LONG BATTLE
ALL CIVILIZATIONS AND MANY UNIVERSES
WERE COMPLETELY DESTROYED.

MEMORIES
OF THOSE WHO DIED GALACTIC AGES AGO
CRY IN MY CELLS:
"FIGHT"...
TIME WAS WHEN ALL THOUGHT THE FIGHT WOULD BE EVEN AGAINST THE ENEMY.
THE FEDERATION DISPATCHED ITS VANGUARD TO THE LIGHT'S YONDER.
IT VANISHED.

FATIGUE,
SOMETHING THAT FOR LONG I'D
FORGOTTEN...

BUT SOON
THEY WILL BE HERE.

I SHALL WATCH HOW THEY INVADE THIS PLANET

AND THUS GRASP THEIR... TRUE NATURE.

I DO NOT WISH TO FIGHT ANYMORE.
'TIS SO I MAY REST IN PEACE.

IS THAT THE STAR THE KING DISCOVERED?

YES... IF IT'S INDEED A FINE NEW STAR,

HE WISHES IT TO BE NAMED "LILIA" AFTER THE QUEEN.

BUT IF IT'S A STAR, THEN IT'S...

IF WE WORKED IT THROUGH THE CASTLE'S THOUGHT-MACHINE, WE'D KNOW RIGHT AWAY,

BUT ALL COSMIC THINGS ARE OF THE MYS-TERIOUS DIVINE—

NOT FOR MAN TO KNOW.

I HOPE IT'S NOT A BAD OMEN.

ODDLY, AFTER THAT NIGHT
THE STAR WAS SEEN NO MORE IN THE SKY.
THEY HAD NO WAY OF KNOWING WHAT THIS FORETOLD.
IT'S DAY-BREAK. LET'S GET GOING!
WHY, IT'S STILL DARK OUT.
STOP WHINING
REAL CARAVANS SET OUT IN THE DARK!
NOW LOOK.
THE SUN IS RISING AS WE SPEAK.
?
AS...
WE
...
AHH !!!

WHA ...
WHAT'S THAT LIGHT?!

ズ
ズ
ズ
ズ
THE LIGHT THAT TURNED DAWN INTO NOON BARELY CLEARED A CREST
BEFORE IT FELL.
IT'S SAID THE IMPACT'S BLAST RAISED A GORGEOUS AURORA
THAT HUNG A WHILE IN THE TWILIT SKY...

KALA PLATEAU CLEARED ...
WE'RE CLOSE.
RESUMING FILMING FROM YESTERDAY. READY FOR TRANS-MISSION.
SPARROW 1 OF THE SURVEY BUREAU CALLING SPARROW 2.
THIS IS SPARROW 2, HEARING. ALTITUDE, 500. THE VIEW'S GREAT!

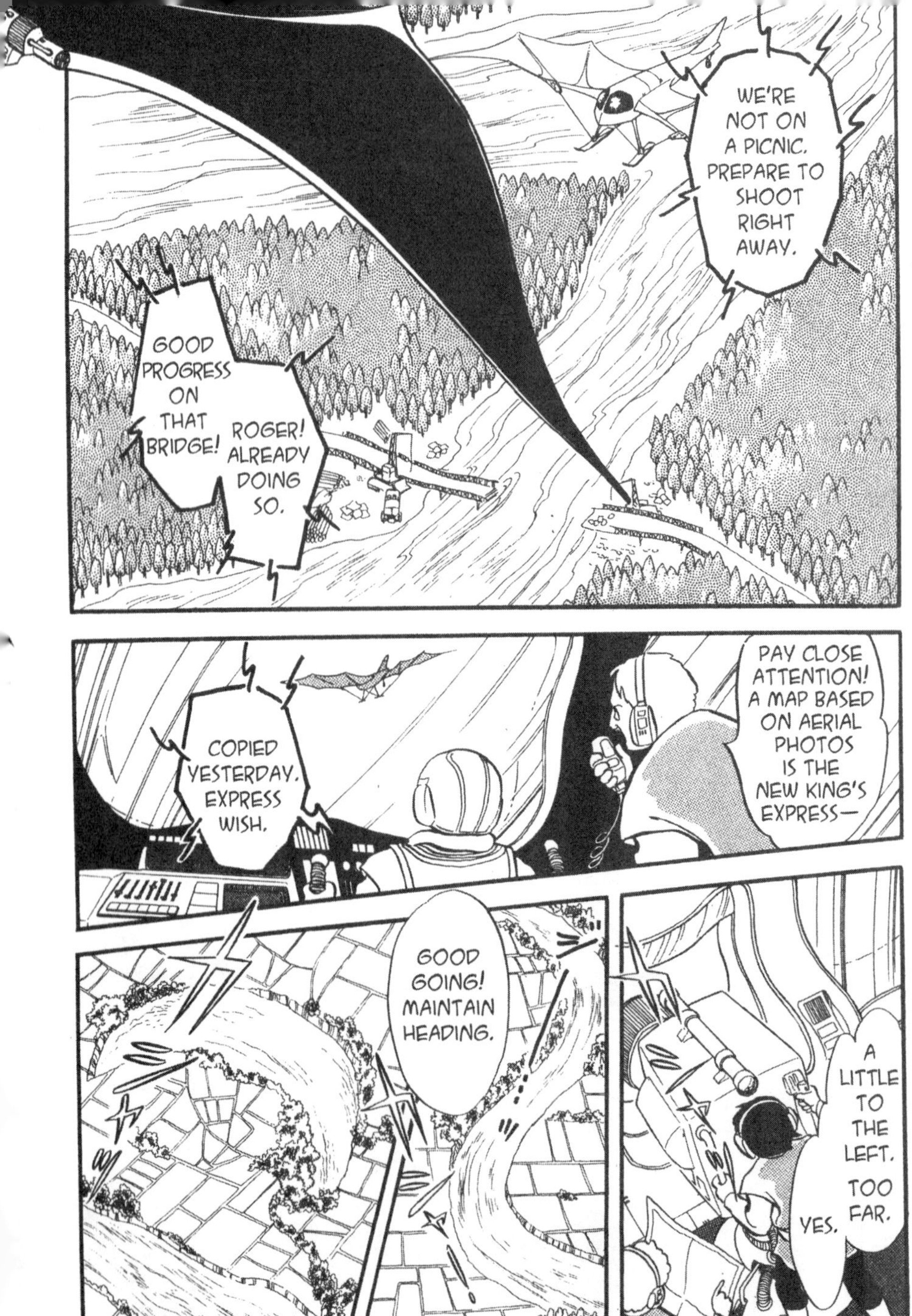

WE'RE NOT ON A PICNIC. PREPARE TO SHOOT RIGHT AWAY.

GOOD PROGRESS ON THAT BRIDGE!

ROGER! ALREADY DOING SO.

PAY CLOSE ATTENTION! A MAP BASED ON AERIAL PHOTOS IS THE NEW KING'S EXPRESS—

COPIED YESTERDAY. EXPRESS WISH.

GOOD GOING! MAINTAIN HEADING.

A LITTLE TO THE LEFT.

TOO FAR.

YES.

CLEAR VISIBILITY. FILMING ON PACE.
WE'LL HEAD NORTH NEXT.
ROGER!
BUT WHAT A BOLD IDEA FROM THE KING! I'M SURE THE ASTROLOGISTS GAVE HIM AN EARFUL.
COMPARED TO NEIGHBORING REALMS WE'RE PRETTY FAR ADVANCED.
IN THE END YOU CAN'T STOP PROGRESS.
THEY PROTESTED QUITE A BIT WHEN THE FORMER KING INSTALLED A THOUGHT-MACHINE...
BUT FINALLY SETTLED FOR LIMITED USE.

IT'S A...
MASSIVE CALDERA !!

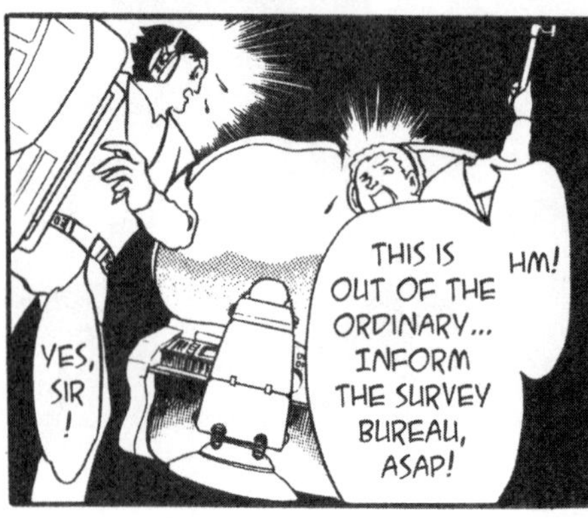

SOMETHING HOT THAT MELTED THE ROCK AS WELL.
SIGNS OF SOMETHING DRAGGING THROUGH THE TREES—
SPARROW 1 TO SURVEY BUREAU! REPORTING A GIGANTIC METEOR CRATER, NORTHEAST OF KALA PLATEAU.
URGENT, REQUEST INVESTI-GATION.
THE EXACT LOCATION IS—
THE TRACE LEADS INTO THE WOODS. SOURCE INVIS-IBLE FROM UP HERE.

THAT WAY

A SEARCH UNIT OF THIS LAND...
FUTILE.
THOSE WHO ONLY KNOW PEACE CAN'T BEGIN TO FACE THEIR HOSTILITY.

THERE IT IS !

ONE MORE BLAST!

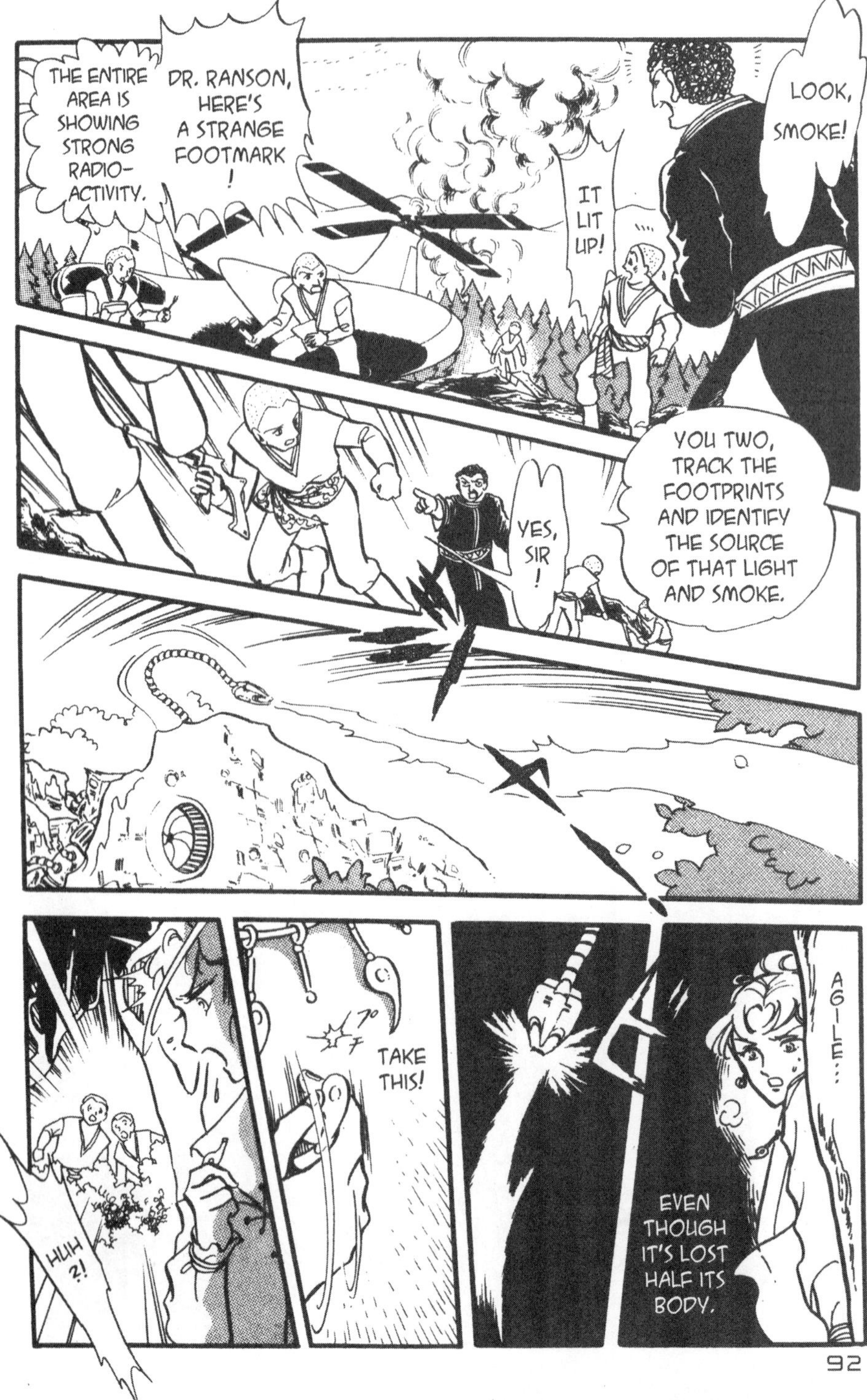
THE ENTIRE AREA IS SHOWING STRONG RADIO-ACTIVITY.
DR. RANSON, HERE'S A STRANGE FOOTMARK!
IT LIT UP!
LOOK, SMOKE!
YOU TWO, TRACK THE FOOTPRINTS AND IDENTIFY THE SOURCE OF THAT LIGHT AND SMOKE.
YES, SIR!
HUH?!
TAKE THIS!
AGILE...
EVEN THOUGH IT'S LOST HALF ITS BODY.

IDIOTS, GO AWA—

AAAARGH

DAMN!

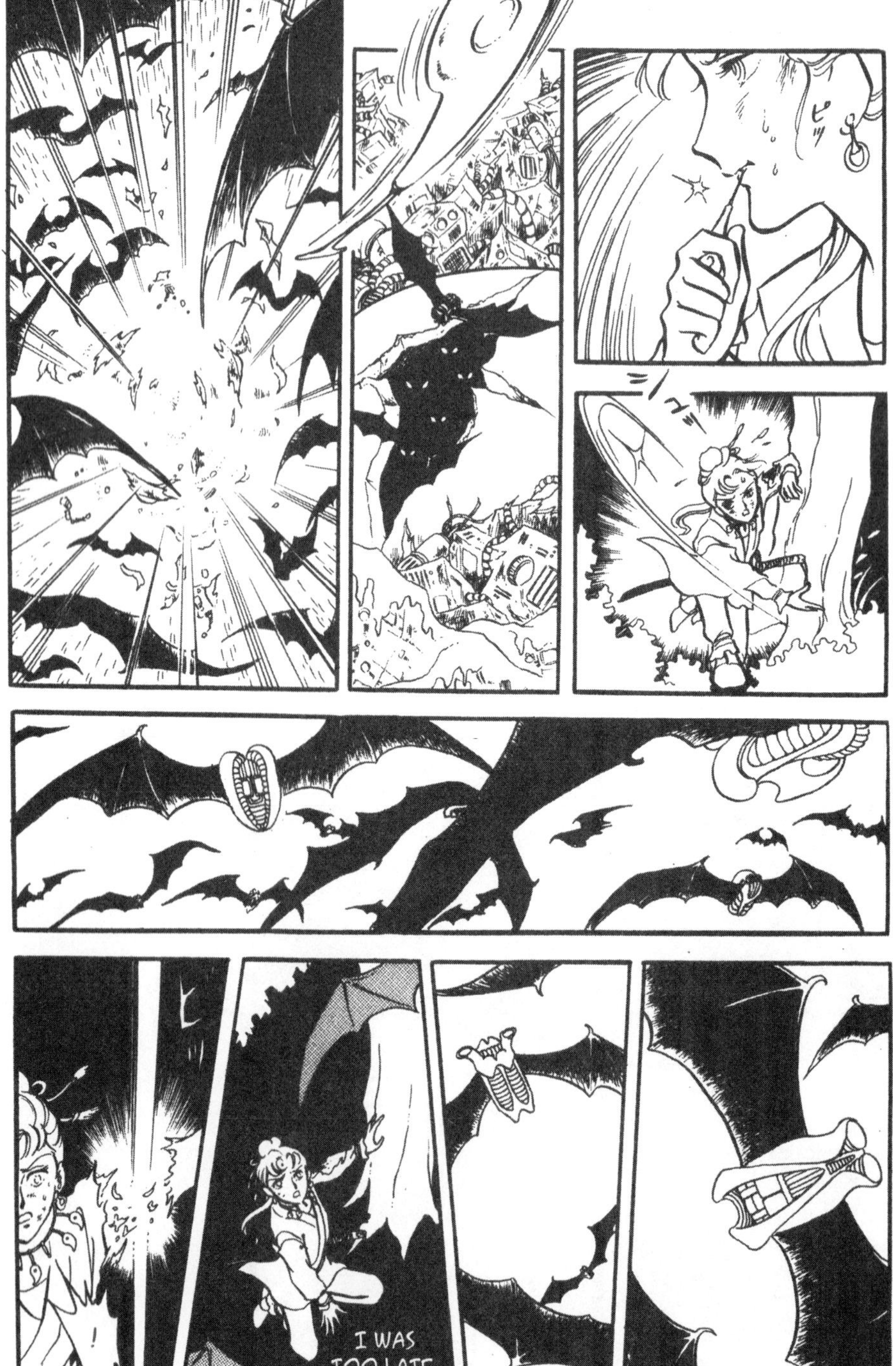
I WAS TOO LATE.

DOCTOR, A SWARM OF BATS, TOWARDS THE CAPITAL ...
NO, IT WAS SOME WEIRD BIRD.
DR., THE TWO!
THEY'RE DEAD!

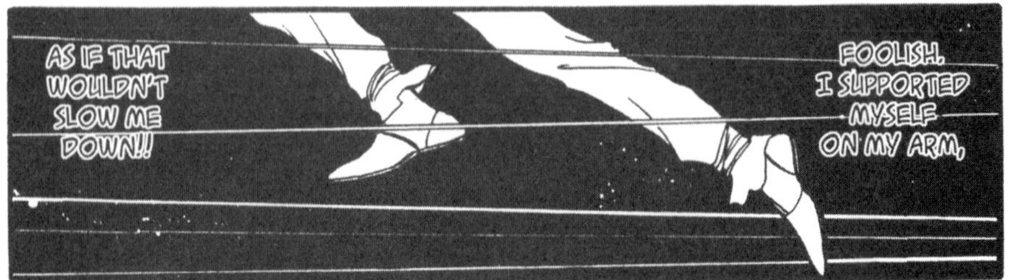
FOOLISH. I SUPPORTED MYSELF ON MY ARM,
AS IF THAT WOULDN'T SLOW ME DOWN!!

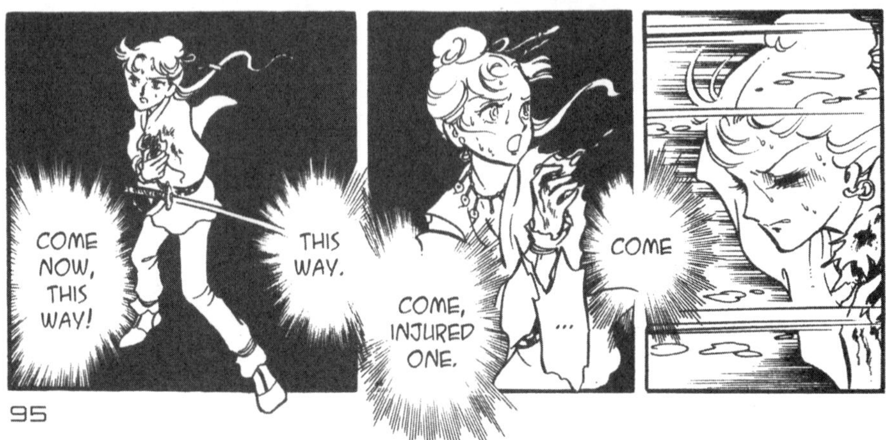
COME
...
COME, INJURED ONE.
THIS WAY.
COME NOW, THIS WAY!

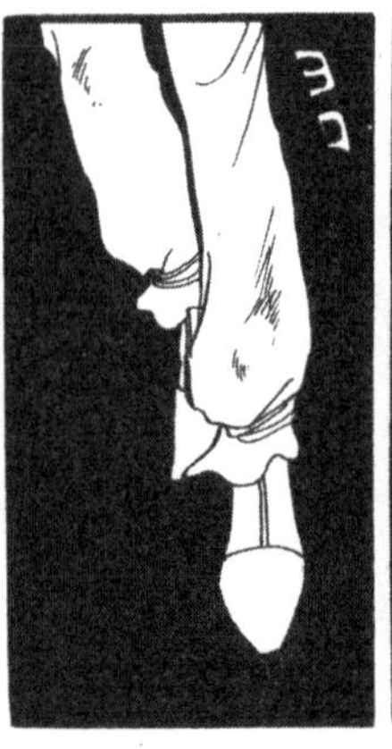

AH
YOU'RE THE ONE WHO'S HURT?

COME ...

AH

QUITE PLEASANT, THE SOUND OF A LOOM.

OR RATHER, IS IT BECAUSE THE BEST IN AYODOYA WEAVES?

NAY... IT IS THE LOOM—MADE BY MY HOMELAND'S GREATEST MASTER.

KING, YOU ARE TRULY FORTUNATE.
THE CLOTH SHE WEAVES FETCHES THE HIGHEST PRICES BACK HOME.
THE TOP LUSTER, AND QUALITY—IT WAS EVEN SAID TO BE FRAGRANT. NEVER ENOUGH TO GO AROUND.
TARAMA!
AND, MY PRINCESS, FOR WHOM DO YOU WEAVE THIS?
HUH?
IT'S A ROBE... FOR MY LORD THE KING.
I PROMISED MYSELF IT WOULD BE THE FIRST THING I'D WEAVE HERE.
LILIA
I KNOW NOT HOW TO MAKE SUCH A GIFT,
BUT I VOUCH YOU THE LAND'S PEACE AND PROSPERITY.
MY LORD!

ALL THAT'S LEFT IS TO WAIT FOR THE BIRTH OF AN HEIR.
WILL THE CHILD HAVE COSMO-RALIA'S DARK HAIR
OR AYODOYA'S RED?!
THAT'S ALL WE TALK ABOUT.
LADIES!
LILIA, IT WOULD NOT MATTER...
A CHILD WITH DARK EYES AND FIERY RED HAIR WOULD PROVE OUR COUNTRIES' BOND!
STRETCH
WE'RE ALMOST DONE FOR THE DAY. SQUARE'S EMPTY, TOO.
A LOT OF BATS TODAY...
WAIT... HOW ODD! THEY'RE ALL FLYING INTO THE WINDOW.

THAT WINDOW, I'VE NEVER SEEN IT OPEN.
I BET A LADY IN WAITING FORGOT AFTER AIRING A RUG.

MAYBE WE OUGHT TO ALERT THE GUARDS.
LET IT BE. BATS NEED A PLACE TO SLEEP, TOO.

HELLO, HELLO,
IS THIS SECU-RITY?
ALL CLEAR HERE IN THE THOUGHT-MACHINE ROOM. JUST ME AND MY BUDDY, WHO'S RESTING.

STRANGE BATS? HAVEN'T SEEN ANYTHING OF THE SORT. ALL RIGHT, OPENING THE DOOR.

ふぁ

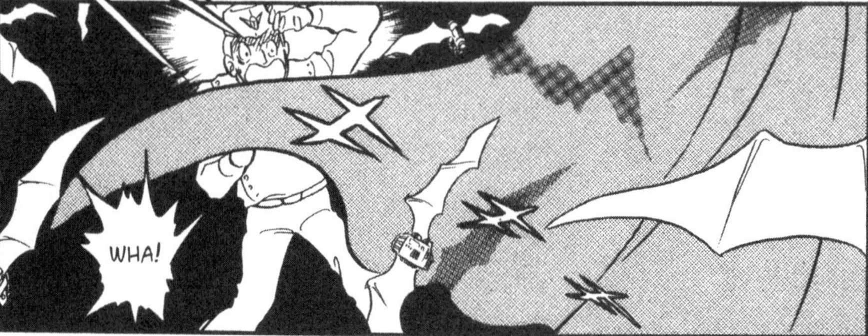
WHA!

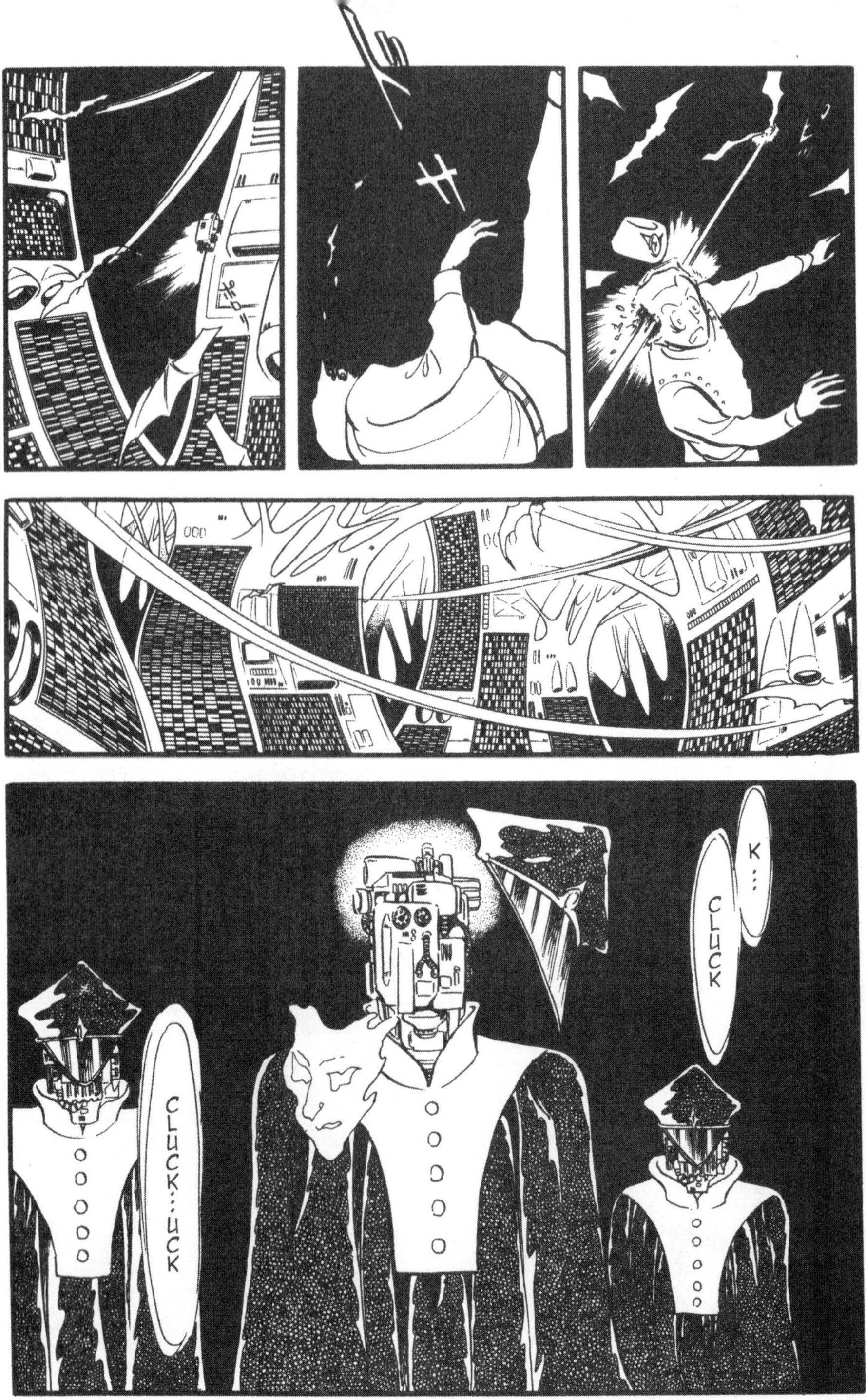

CLUCK…UCK

K…

CLUCK

ザワ…
ザワ
ザワ

THAT'S RIGHT!
THEN THEY WENT TO CHECK OUT THE CALDERA
THERE
AND TWO GUYS GOT KILLED, BRUTALLY, BY SOME WEIRD THING.
DID YOU HEAR LUMA'S BOYFRIEND IS MISSING?
THE THOUGHT-MACHINE TECHNICIAN, RIGHT?
YEAH!
WE TRIED TO INVESTIGATE, BUT SINCE IT'S THAT ROOM, THEY WOULDN'T EVEN LET US IN.
THEY HAD THIS GLAZED LOOK AND SPOKE IN A FLAT VOICE
AS IF... THEY WERE DEMONS READY TO EAT ME ALIVE!

GE...
GET OUT.
STAY AWAY.
STAY AWAY.
GET OUT.
ST...
HUSH NOW!
THE QUEEN CAN HEAR YOU!!
Y...
YES.

PARDON THEM, MY QUEEN.
LET IT BE.
WHEN PEOPLE NEED TO TALK, THEY WILL.
STILL... HOW EERIE...
HM?
THE TECHNICIANS?
NOT TO WORRY, LILIA. I'LL HAVE THEM LOOK INTO IT
SO NOT ONE THING IN THIS LAND CAN VEX YOU!
WHY, AS LOVEY-DOVEY AS EVER!
BUT WORDS ARE FREE, AREN'T THEY.

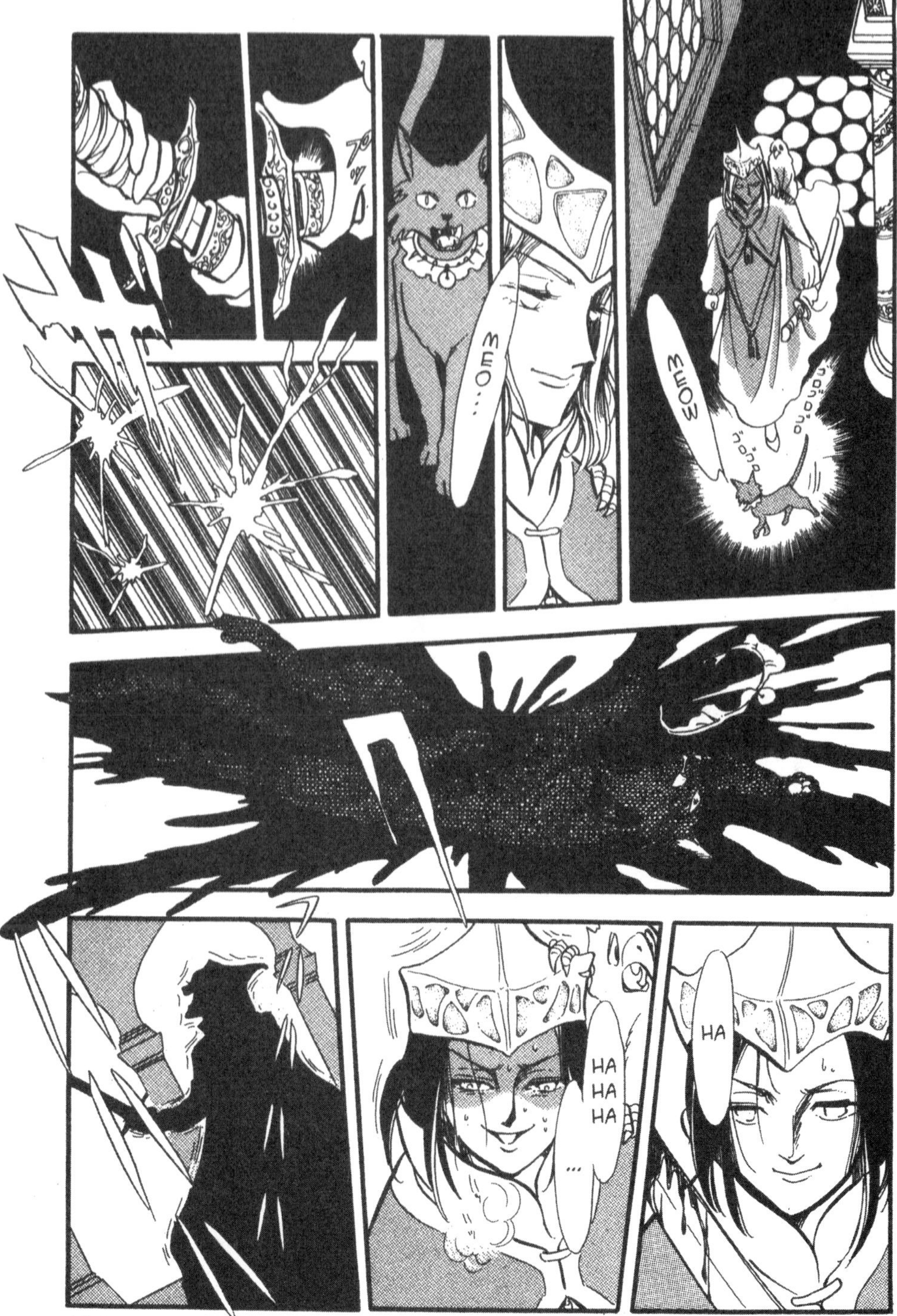
MEOW
ゴロゴロゴロ
ゴロゴロ
MEO...
フッ
HA
HA
HA
HA
...

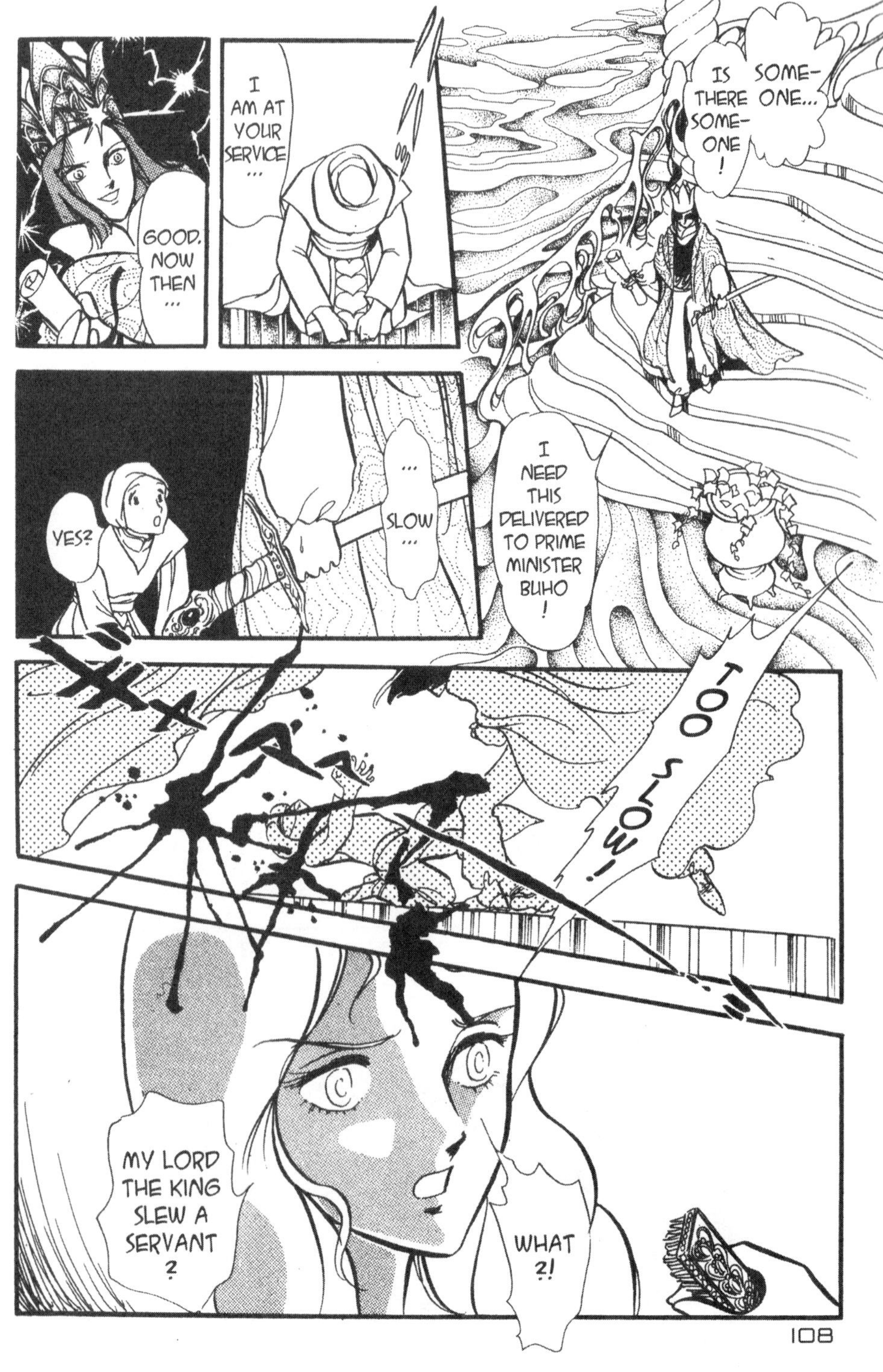
IS THERE SOME-ONE SOME-ONE...!
I AM AT YOUR SERVICE...
GOOD, NOW THEN...
I NEED THIS DELIVERED TO PRIME MINISTER BUHO!
YES?
...SLOW...
TOO SLOW!
MY LORD THE KING SLEW A SERVANT?
WHAT?!

MY QUEEN... SOMETHING MUST HAVE REALLY CAUGHT HIS MAJESTY'S IRE!
THE HORROR...
BUT HE IS SO KIND...
WHAT'S THE MATTER?
NOTHING
IT'S GOOD OF YOU TO COME.
THERE, I HAVE FINISHED YOUR ROBE...

HE'S AS HAPPY AS A CHILD...
WHAT IN THE WORLD COULD HAVE...
AH ...
LILIA!
A HEARTFELT GIFT— I SHALL CHERISH IT BETTER THAN ANY RICHES!
PLEASE! KING!
AHH!
IT HURTS
MY LORD,
NOT SO TIGHT ...

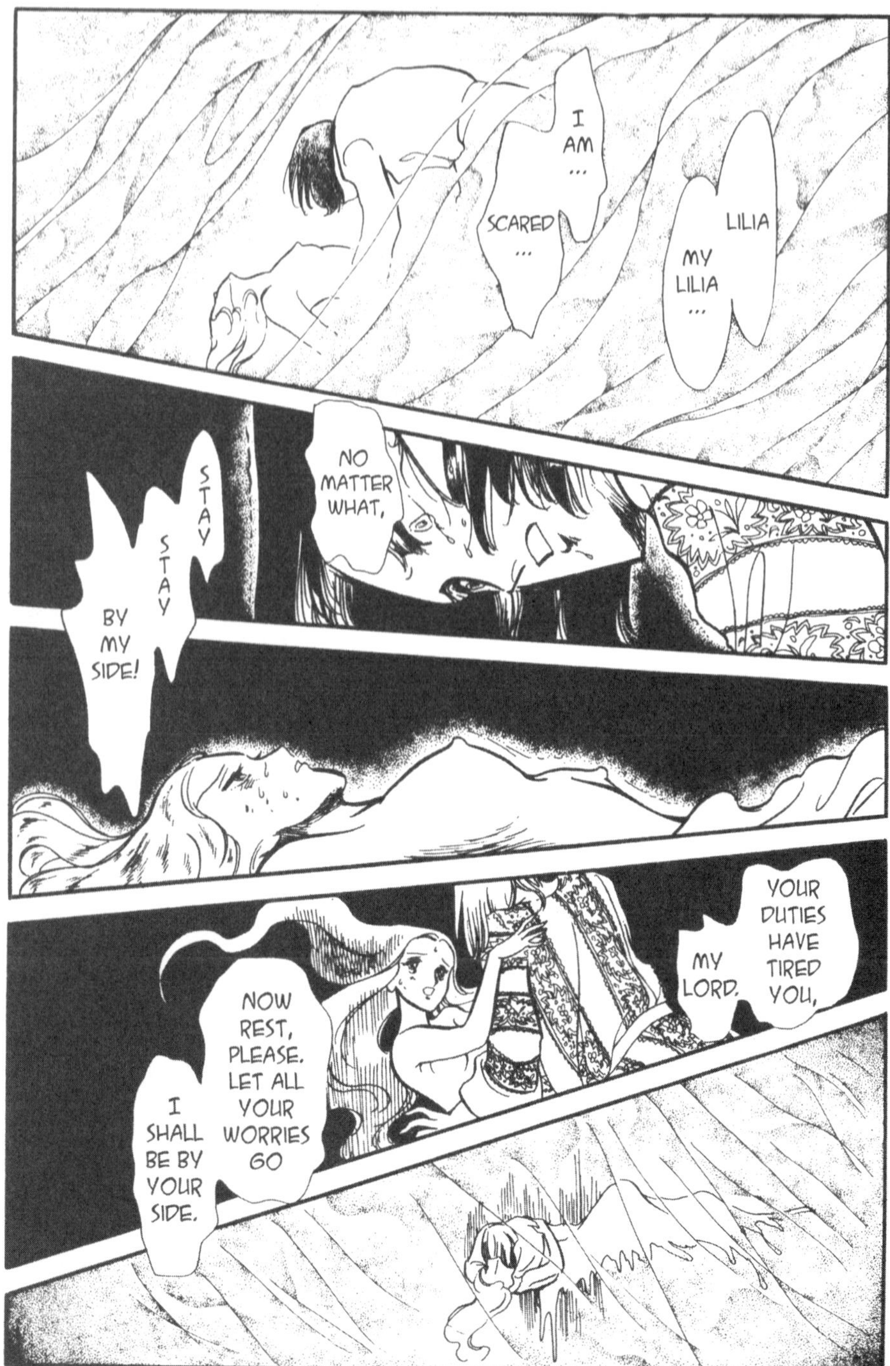
LILIA
MY LILIA ...
I AM ...
SCARED ...
NO MATTER WHAT,
STAY
STAY
BY MY SIDE!
YOUR DUTIES HAVE TIRED YOU,
MY LORD.
NOW REST, PLEASE. LET ALL YOUR WORRIES GO
I SHALL BE BY YOUR SIDE.

NIGHT!
WHERE ARE YOU?
YOU THERE, HAVE YOU SEEN THE CAT?
IT'S BEEN GONE FOR 3 DAYS.
THAT'S ODD.
IT'S NEVER BEEN AWAY FROM ME THIS LONG.
QUEEN! PRINCESS LILIA!!

POOR, POOR NIGHT.
MY BROTHER HAD HIM SENT TO ME BECAUSE HE WAS CRYING FOR ME.
WELL, DOCTOR? WHAT DO YOU SAY?
SHE'S WITH CHILD.
WITH...
HEAR YE,
HER ROYAL MAJESTY HAS CON- CEIVED!

NURSE?

TARAMA...

I AM NOT A GOOD CONSORT, TARAMA! I SUSPECT THE KING ...
SUSPECT THAT HE KILLED MY CAT!
BUT WHY WOULD HE?!
I WISH I AGREED. BUT HE'S BEEN ACTING SO STRANGE LATELY.
OH!
HIS ARMS THAT HELD ME FELT... LIKE A MACHINE!!
HEAR ME THIS ONCE, AND
SEND FOR MY BROTHER. I COULD ONLY EVER TRUST HIM!
NO! THAT WILL ONLY MAKE MATTERS WORSE !
ALL RIGHT THEN.
I'LL ARRANGE A VISIT. HE CAN COME TO CELEBRATE YOUR CONCEPTION.

AYODOYA
AH, IS THAT SO?!
SUCH GOOD NEWS.
DRINKS ALL AROUND ON THE PALACE TONIGHT!

AND THIS IS A LETTER FROM NURSE TARAMA.
HMM...
WHAT?!
LILIA'S WITH CHILD?
YES— COSMORALIA MUST BE SEETHING WITH EXCITEMENT NOW.
FATHER!
A JOYOUS OCCASION, BUT I AM OLD.
AS REGENT, PAY HER A VISIT IN MY STEAD TO CONGRATULATE HER.
YES, SIR!
THAT IS ALL.
STRANGE—
THAT LOYAL TARAMA, ASKING SPECIFICALLY FOR MILAN...

WALK...

I WANT TO SLEEP.

WALK.

NO, I CAN'T.
WHO DRAGS ME?

WALK!

I'M IN PAIN!

ARE YOU ... ASTRA?

TO SO COERCE A KING?

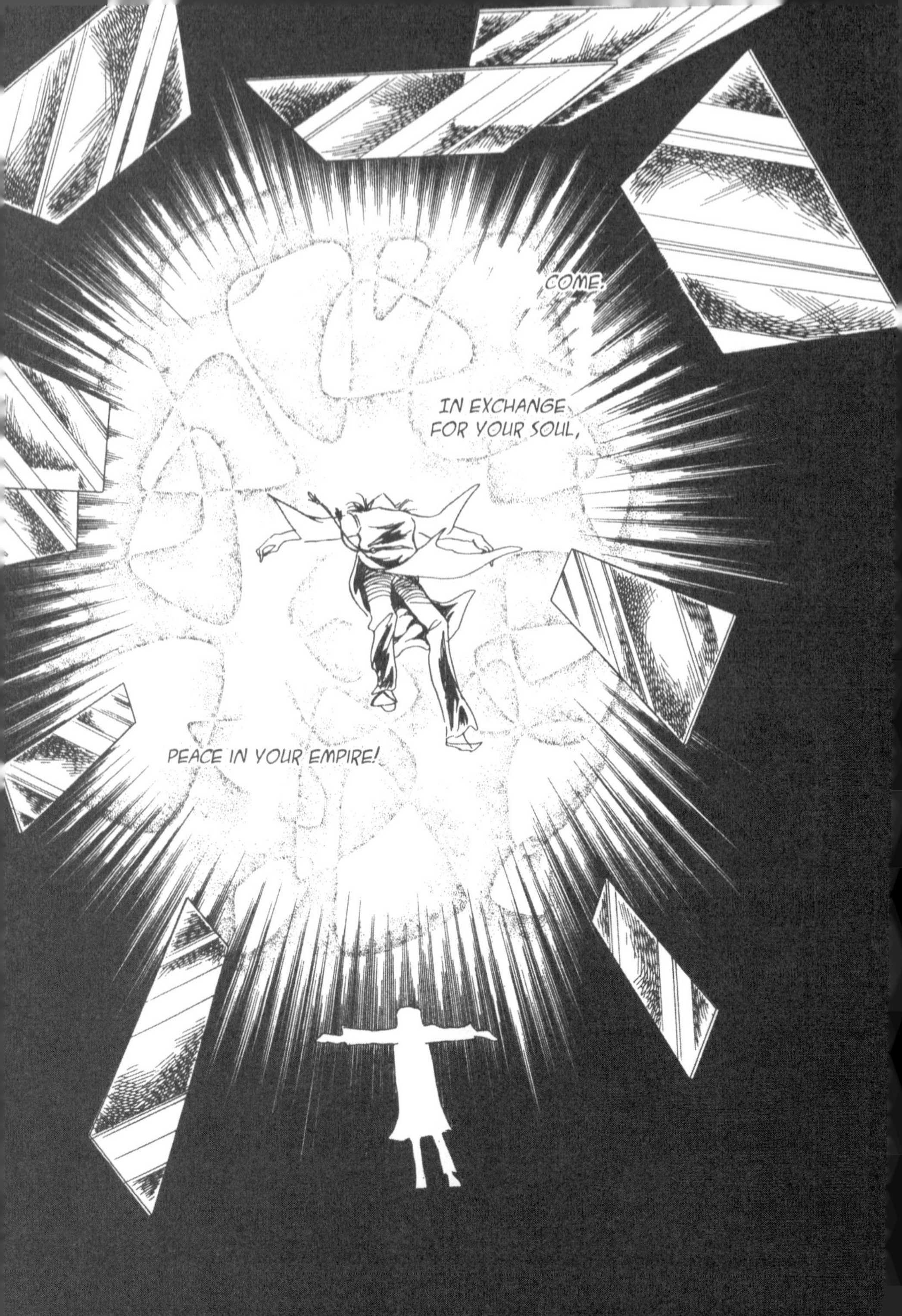
COME.
IN EXCHANGE FOR YOUR SOUL,
PEACE IN YOUR EMPIRE!

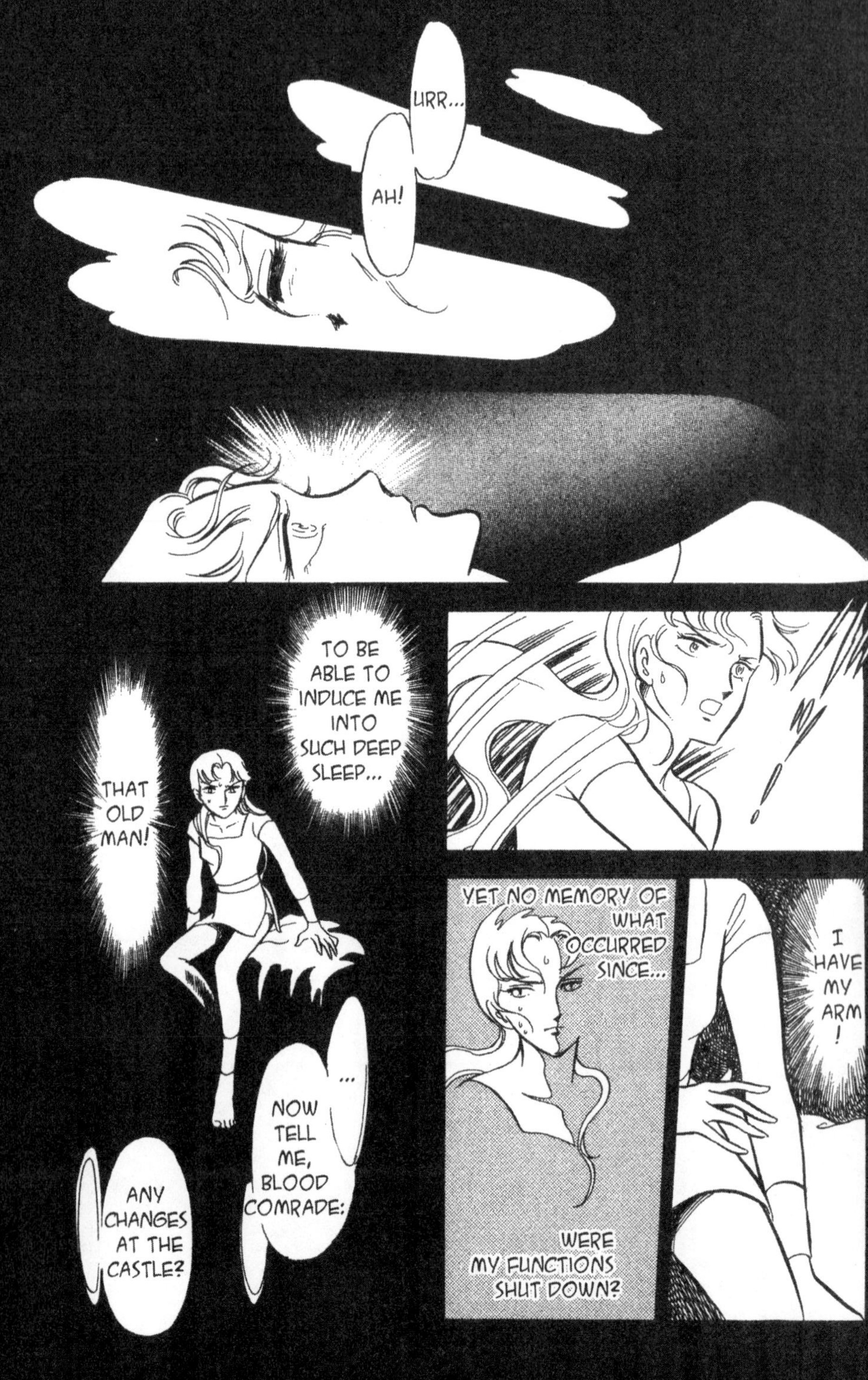

URR...
AH!
I HAVE MY ARM!
YET NO MEMORY OF WHAT OCCURRED SINCE...
WERE MY FUNCTIONS SHUT DOWN?
TO BE ABLE TO INDUCE ME INTO SUCH DEEP SLEEP...
THAT OLD MAN!
...
NOW TELL ME, BLOOD COMRADE:
ANY CHANGES AT THE CASTLE?

AH HA...

EVER SINCE THAT STAR FELL, BIZARRE THINGS HAPPEN THERE?

YES.

THE THOUGHT-MACHINE ROOM, FORMERLY OPEN, IS NOW STRICTLY OFF-LIMITS, AND...

MOST OF THE STAFF'S BEEN FIRED.

"BLOOD COMRADE"?

THEN WHO RUNS THE THING NOW?

I HAVE NO CLUE.

BUT THE FACT IS WATER AND ELECTRICITY AREN'T BEING SUPPLIED PROPERLY TO THE REALM.

THERE HAVE BEEN DIRECT APPEALS TO THE KING,

BUT HE'S NOT HIMSELF AND WILL NOT HEAR.

SHH!

MY GUEST... RATHER THAN EAVESDROP, COME OUT AND QUERY 'TIL YOU'RE SATED.

ガタッ!

WHO'S HERE ?!

FRIEND OR FOE? WRONG ANSWER AND YOU DIE.
STAND DOWN, GODAI!
SHE'S NOT A FOE, BUT A WARRIOR THAT THEY WOUNDED. SHE NEEDS TO REST.
I'LL BET SHE MOUNTED AN INITIAL DEFENSE AGAINST THEM
AND IS GRITTING HER TEETH AT THEIR ENORMITY AND BRUTALITY.
ISN'T THAT SO, MY GUEST?

HMPH! YOU SPEAK AS IF YOU KNOW THEIR TRUE NATURE.

NO, I DO NOT ...
...ARE YOU...
ALONE?
...!

I DON'T OWE YOU WORDS. I'M NOT OF THIS PLACE
AND THE ENEMY IS MY ONLY INTEREST. SORRY.
YOU CAN'T FIGHT ALONE.
IT'D BE FUTILE, ESPECIALLY WITH A BODY LIKE YOURS.

YOUR TORN-OFF ARM GROWS IN AS FLESH
BUT YOU'LL NEED SOME REST BEFORE BLOOD COURSES THROUGH IT FULLY.

YOU'RE... A GOOD DOCTOR. THERE SHOULD BE NO NEED.
I'D LIKE TO LEAVE HERE SOON.
IS THAT SO...

TOO BAD WE CAN'T TOUCH THIS DIRECTLY— NOT US.
THE WRAP IS MADE OF LEAD!

THEN AS PAYMENT FOR YOUR TREATMENT, I'D LIKE A PIECE OF WHAT'S IN YOUR WAIST POUCH.
!
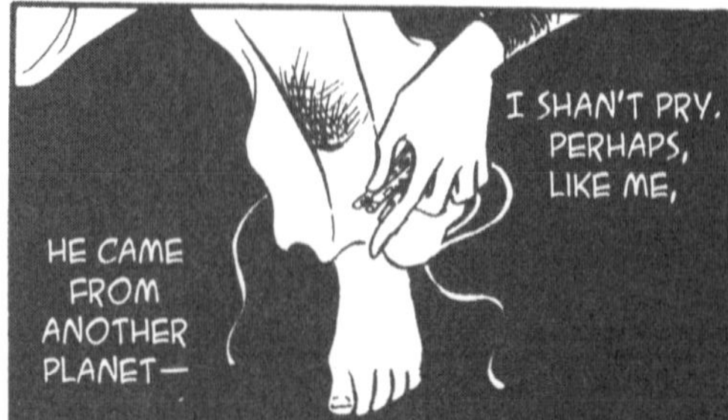
I SHAN'T PRY. PERHAPS, LIKE ME,
HE CAME FROM ANOTHER PLANET—

HE WANTED A RADIOACTIVE ISOTOPE...
WHO— WHAT—IS THAT OLD MAN?!
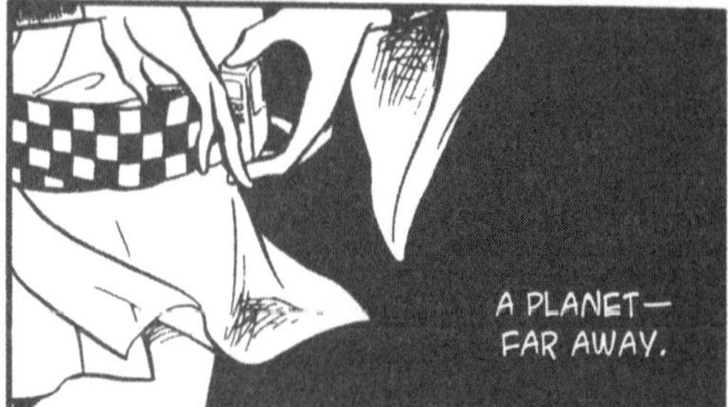
A PLANET— FAR AWAY.

I CAN'T FIGHT ALONE?
I MUST!

WHETHER OR NOT IT'S POSSIBLE.

ALAS, THEY'VE REACHED THIS PLANET ASTRIAS MUCH SOONER THAN US...

OUR FORCES ARE STILL FAR OFF.

IF I DO NOT FIGHT, THEY CONQUER.

THEN WHATEVER THE COST...!

FOR ALLIES WHO MAY NEVER COME?

ONLY THE ROYAL BLOOD OF AYODOYA CAN HALT THEM

YES ...

ONLY THAT BEAUTIFUL QUEEN, AND THE PRINCE TO BE BORN...

I CAN'T MOVE!
IS HE A TELEPATH?
PROTECT
THE
PRINCE TO BE BORN!
YOU'LL FIND OUR KNOW-LEDGE USEFUL.
AS OUR ALLY...
WE NEED YOUR HELP.
STOP IT!

HE'S... THAT FAR?
I FELT HIM RIGHT BEHIND ME.
ARE YOU OKAY?
YOU STILL NEED TO TAKE IT EASY WITH THAT ARM.
HO HO
HUH?!

PRINCE—
HE KNOWS IT WILL BE A BOY?
PRINCE JIMSA—
RIDICULOUS!

WE'LL MEET AGAIN.
YOU CAN HELP ME THEN.

HA... STUBBORN!
BUT ALL WARRIORS OF RODLIAN WERE SO.

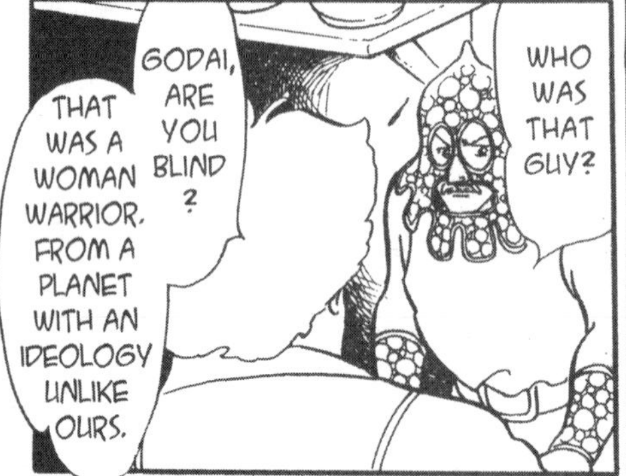
WHO WAS THAT GUY?
GODAI, ARE YOU BLIND?
THAT WAS A WOMAN WARRIOR. FROM A PLANET WITH AN IDEOLOGY UNLIKE OURS.

A WO-MAN?!
WELL, AS YOU SAW, SHE IS VIRTUALLY A MAN.
UNINJURED, SHE BEATS YOU IN BOTH STRENGTH AND SKILL.

...
TIME FOR YOU TO HEAD BACK TO THE CASTLE. WITH YOUR SON BALGA, PROTECT THE AYODOYAN BRIDE.
DON'T LOSE SIGHT OF OUR AIM.

YES, SIR!

!?

RODLIAN WARRIOR,
THEY ARE OUR COMMON ENEMY, BUT WE FIGHT DIFFERENTLY.
RODLIAN WAS DESTROYED BY THEM,

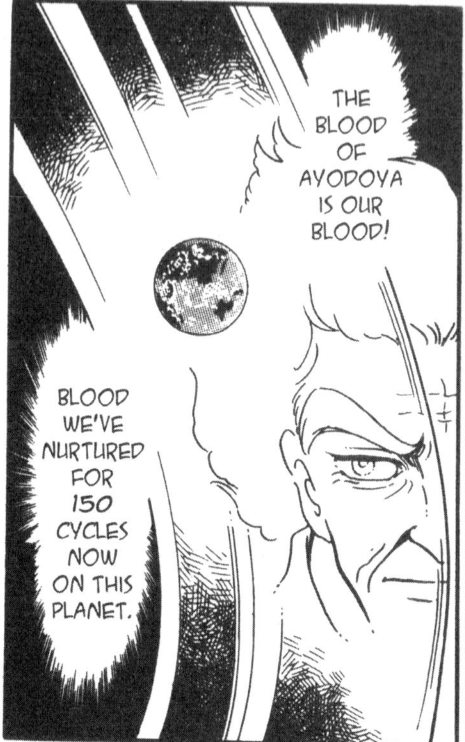
THE BLOOD OF AYODOYA IS OUR BLOOD!
BLOOD WE'VE NURTURED FOR 150 CYCLES NOW ON THIS PLANET.

BUT WE HAVE NOT FALLEN YET
AND SHALL NOT, UNTIL THE LAST DROP OF OUR BLOOD TRICKLES INTO THE GROUND!
DO YOU UNDERSTAND THIS?

WE AREN'T LIKE RODLIAN, WHOSE CIVILIZATION SURVIVED BY LEANING ON MACHINES...
AND THE ENEMY, TOO, WILL KNOW
ONE DAY, THAT MACHINE AND UNIVERSE CAN NEVER CROSS!
シャーン
シャーン
シャーン
LET US CELEBRATE!
THE QUEEN IS WITH CHILD!
DRINK! DANCE!

GET HIM! KILL HIM!
A MATCH IN EARNEST TO CELEBRATE THE QUEEN'S CONCEPTION!
IN THEIR AUGUST PRE-SENCE!
PRINCE MILAN OF THE KINGDOM OF AYODOYA ARRIVES!
MAKE THEM STOP!
I WON'T WATCH THEM RISK THEIR LIVES!
WHY NOT? SEE HOW PLEASED THE PEOPLE ARE.

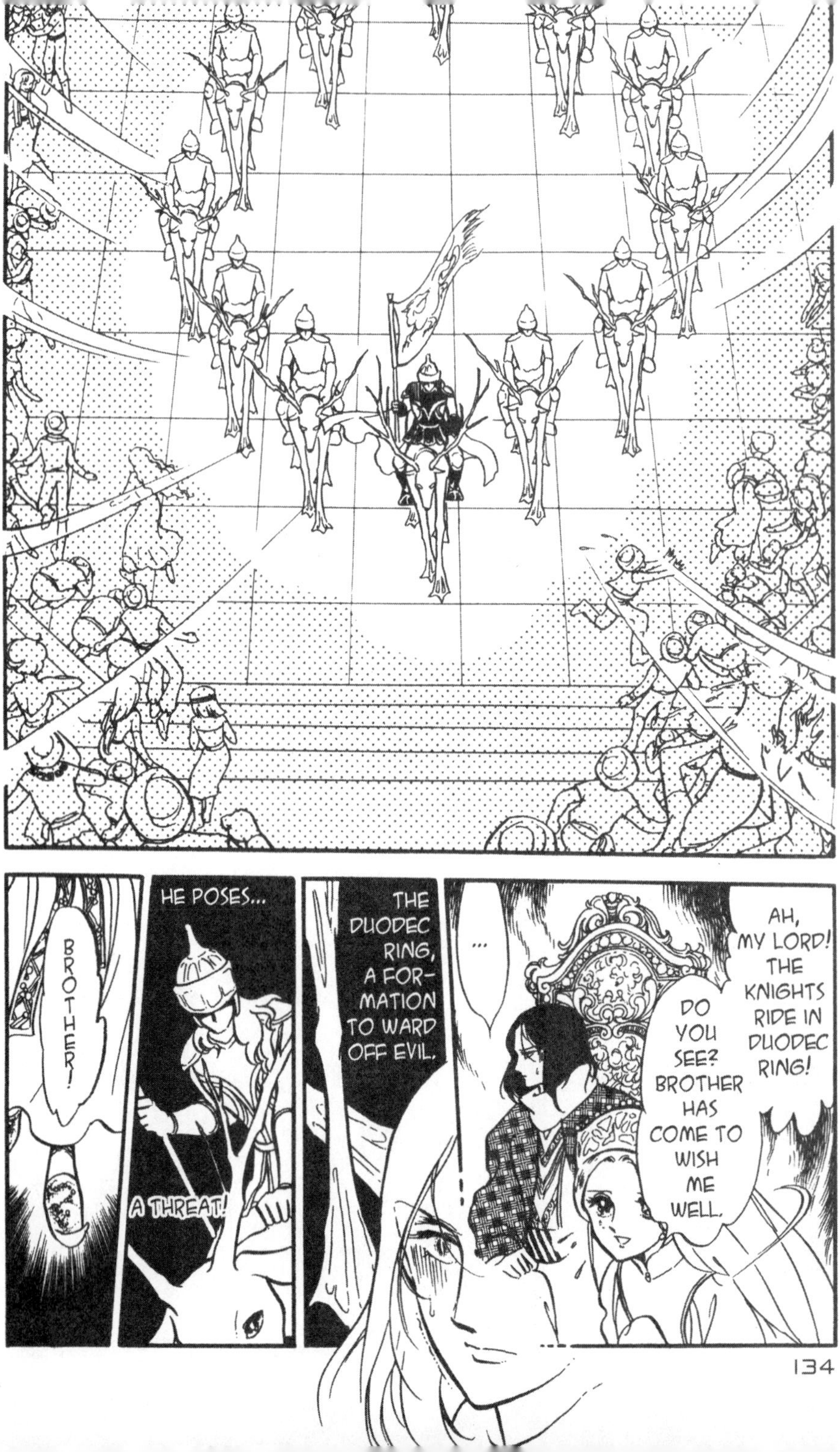

AH, MY LORD! THE KNIGHTS RIDE IN DUODEC RING!
DO YOU SEE? BROTHER HAS COME TO WISH ME WELL.
...
...
THE DUODEC RING, A FORMATION TO WARD OFF EVIL.
HE POSES...
A THREAT!
BROTHER!

GLAD YOU COULD MAKE IT.
CONGRATULATIONS ON THE QUEEN'S CONCEPTION, YOUR MAJESTY. EXCUSE, PLEASE, MY TARDINESS AS I'VE COME TO JOIN IN THE CELEBRATIONS.
NOW CARRY ON! THE FIGHT IS NOT OVER!
WHAT?! A DEATH MATCH?
HAVE THEM CALL IT OFF! THE QUEEN CAN'T STAND IT!

ASTRALTA III, I DIDN'T THINK YOU WERE INTO THAT SORT OF THING.
I KNEW YOU TO BE A KIND MAN AS PRINCE ...
CALL ME ITHACA.
IT WAS ROUGH-HOUSING THAT WENT TOO FAR. DON'T TORMENT ME SO...
WHAT'S ON YOUR MIND?
LILIA DOESN'T LOOK QUITE WELL, EITHER. I'D BE HAPPY TO BE YOUR CONFIDANT.
MILAN! HELP ME! STAY HERE WITH ME!
DON'T GO BACK HOME. YES...
STAY ON AS MY POLITICAL ADVISOR!
ITHACA, THAT'S NOT POS-SIBLE.
NO DOUBT THE CROWN WEIGHS HEAVY ON YOUR HEAD, BUT I, TOO, AM HEIR TO AYODOYA'S THRONE.
THAT'S NOT IT!
MILAN
I...
I...

KING!!

THE DOCTOR SAYS THAT STRONG REPRESSION KICKED IN TO UNDO HIS REASON.

RESTRAINT AND SOME POWERFUL IMPULSE COLLIDED IN HIS MIND.

...

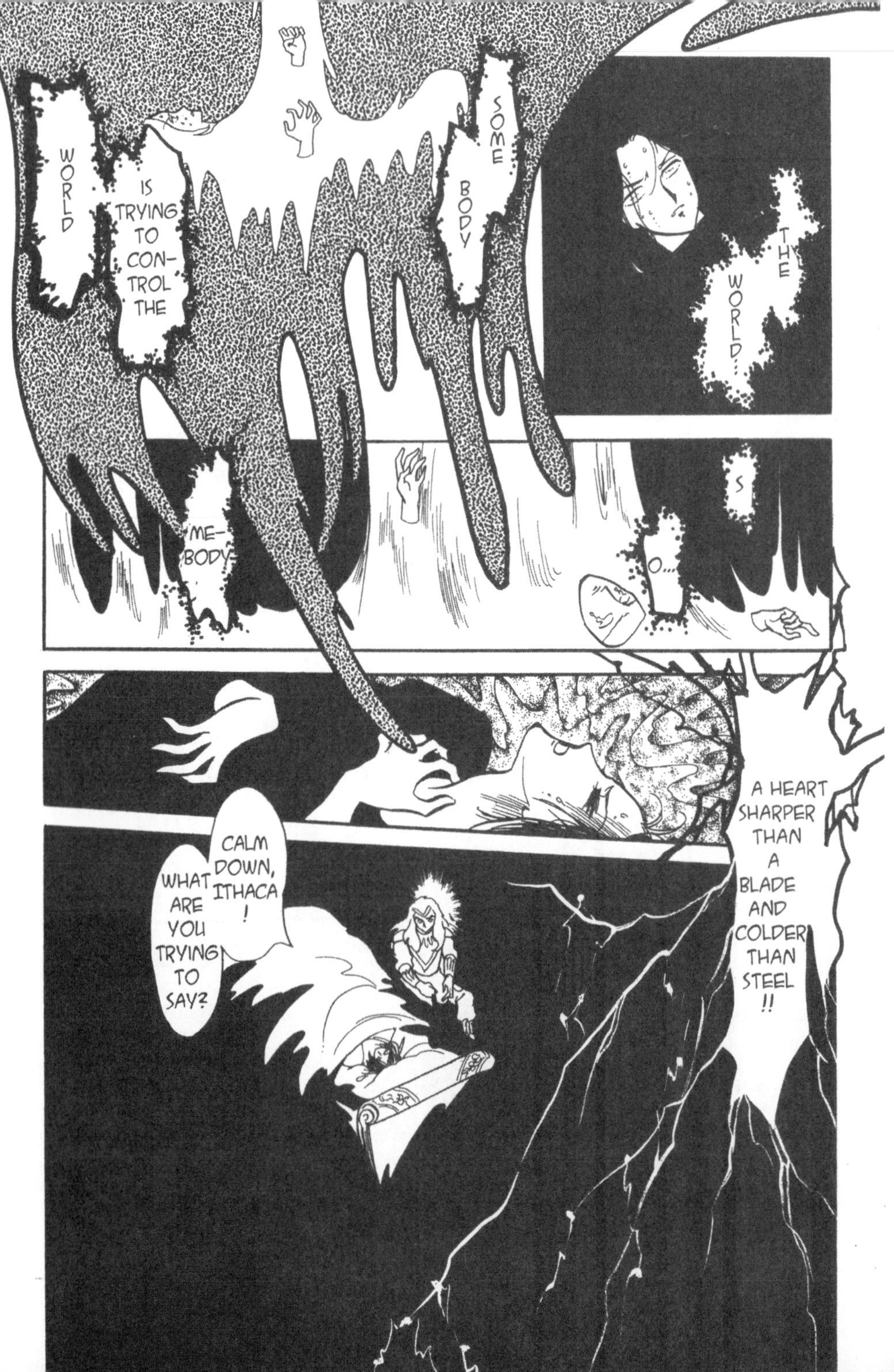
THE WORLD...
SOMEBODY
IS TRYING TO CONTROL THE
WORLD
SO...
ME-BODY
A HEART SHARPER THAN A BLADE AND COLDER THAN STEEL!!
CALM DOWN, ITHACA!
WHAT ARE YOU TRYING TO SAY?

ZZZZZ
HICC
PHEW... LOOKS LIKE I GOT DRUNK AND FELL ASLEEP.
POP'LL KICK MY ASS IF I WALKED IN AT THIS HOUR.
YAWN
GUESS I'LL JUST TAKE A PISS AND GO BACK TO SLEEP.
IT AIN'T EASY HAVING A STRICT PARENT.
HM?
HEY
IT'S THAT GIRL!

I'M TAILING YOU.
BUT SHE IS ACTING STRANGE.
NAH. SHE MIGHT BE STRONG,
BUT THAT'S NOT A BURGLAR'S FACE.
THE SEWER?
WHY?

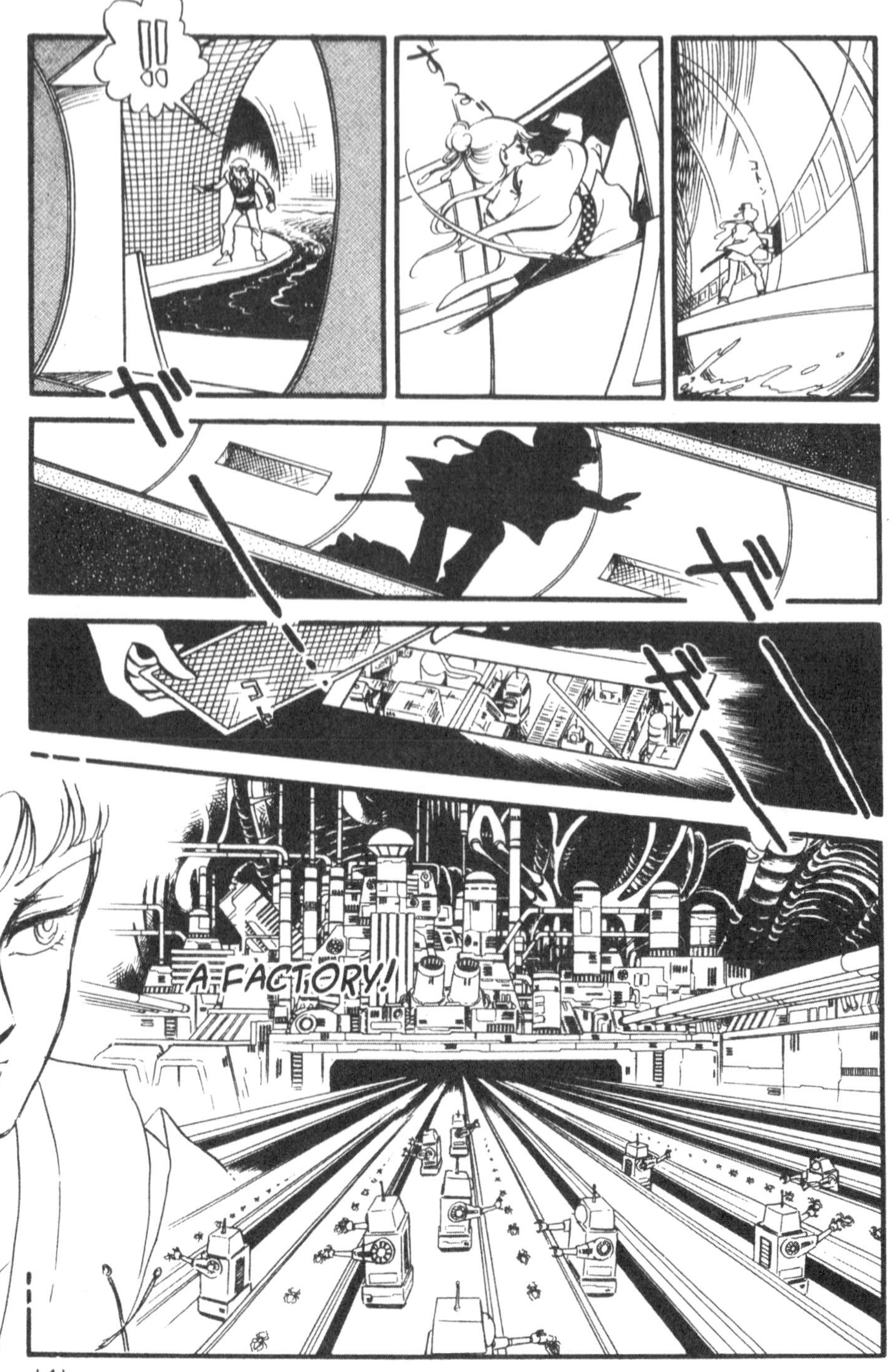
!!
ガ
ガ
A FACTORY!

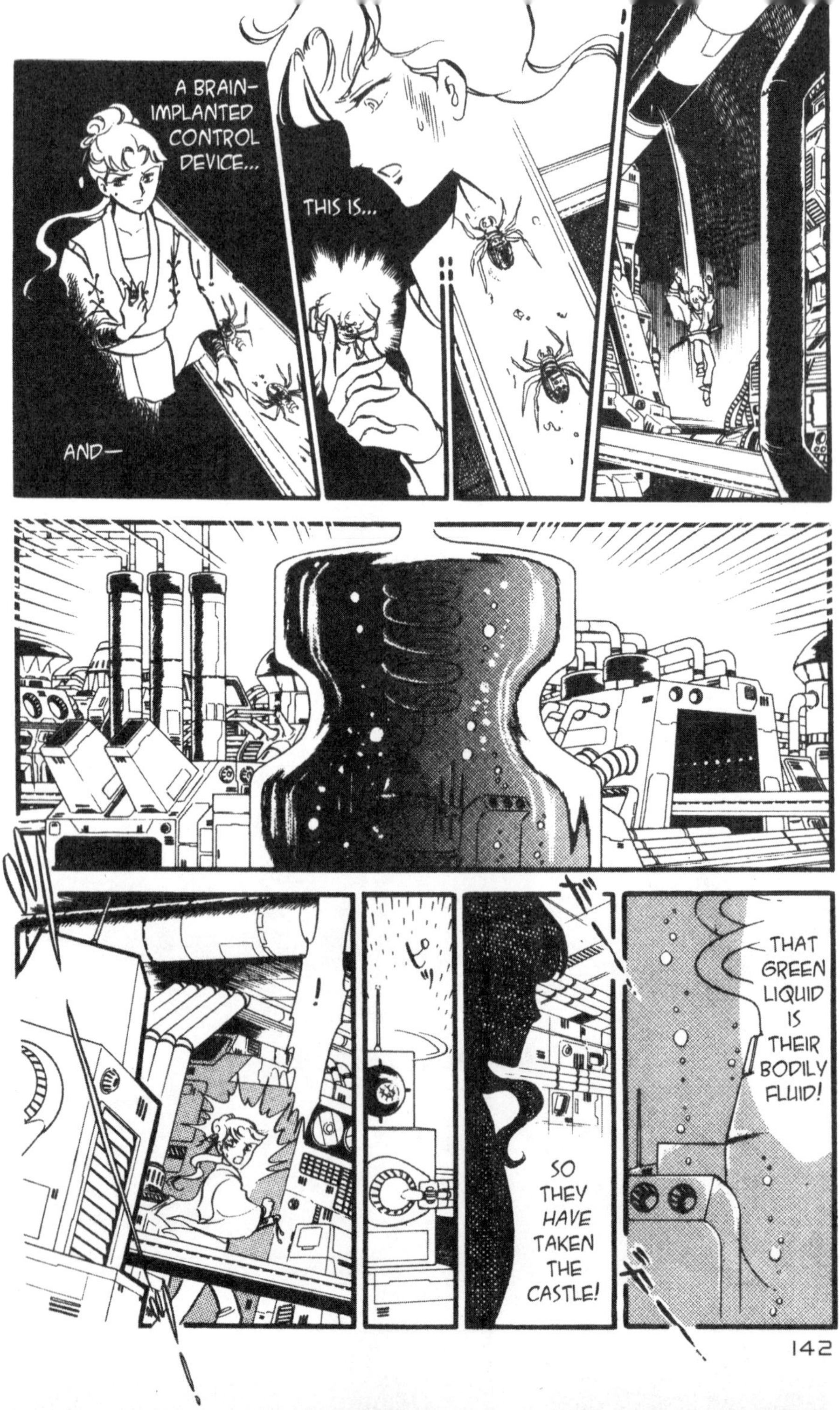

THIS IS...
A BRAIN-IMPLANTED CONTROL DEVICE...
AND—

THAT GREEN LIQUID IS THEIR BODILY FLUID!
SO THEY HAVE TAKEN THE CASTLE!

ピ!
ピ!!

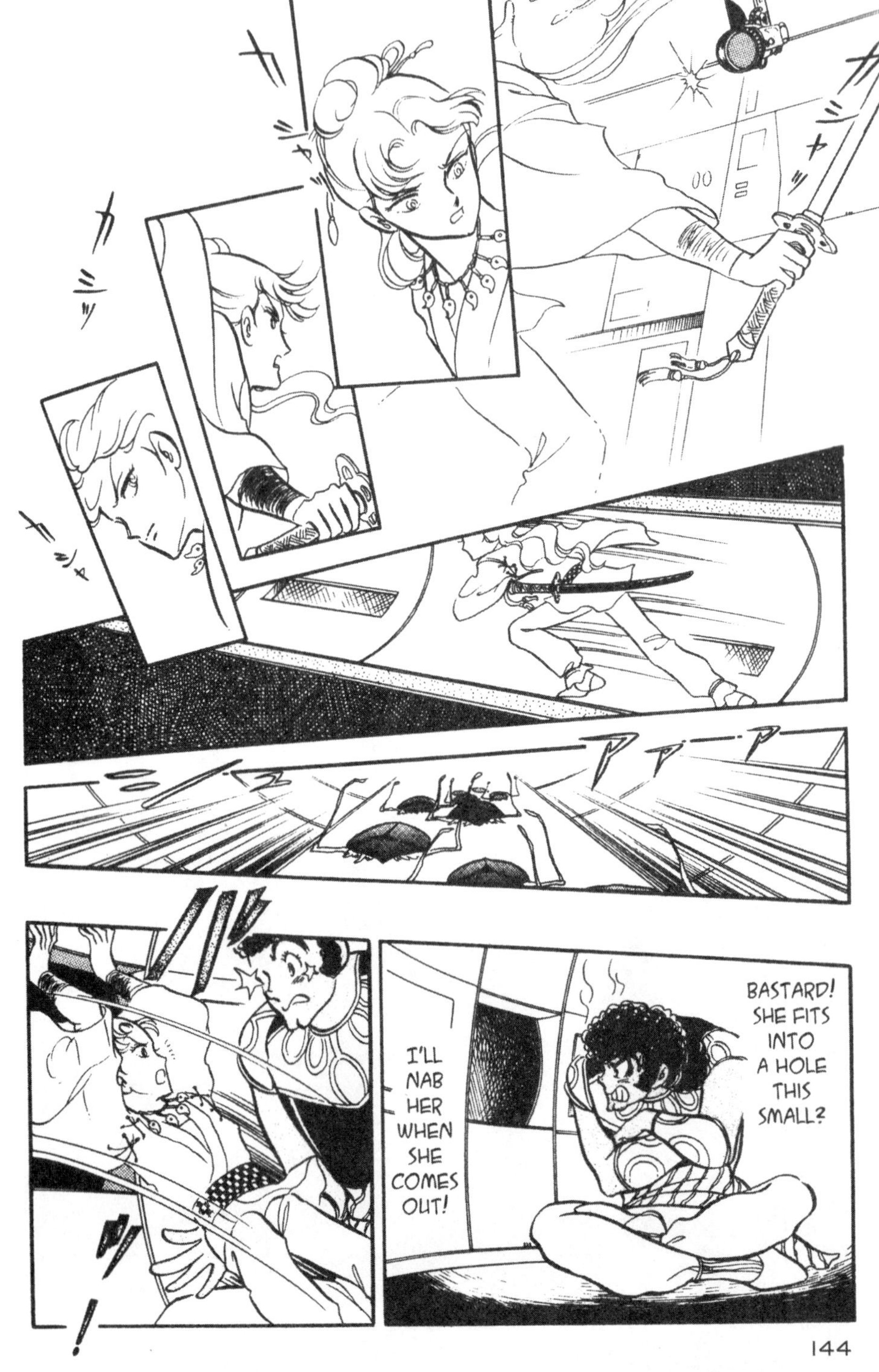
BASTARD! SHE FITS INTO A HOLE THIS SMALL?
I'LL NAB HER WHEN SHE COMES OUT!

CAUGHT A WHITE RAT!
LET GO!
NO WAY. I'VE BEEN LOOKING FOR YOU ALL OVER.
UGH
?
?

GOOD THING THEY WERE OF SIMPLE MAKE.

FIRST TIME YOU'VE SEEN IT?

WHAT THE HELL WAS THAT?

THAT'S WHAT MACHINES BORN OF MACHINES ARE LIKE. THEY ARE ALIVE!

M-MOVING LIKE IT WAS ALIVE...

I...I'VE NEVER SEEN SUCH A MACHINE!

YOU PEACE-HEADS WON'T GET IT, THOUGH ...
GO SEE THE OLD MAN IN THE FOREST IF YOU WANT TO LEARN MORE.
THIS KINGDOM HAS BEEN INFESTED.
THERE'S THE PROOF.
WHA...
...

カサ…コソ
プッ
ズ…
スー…!

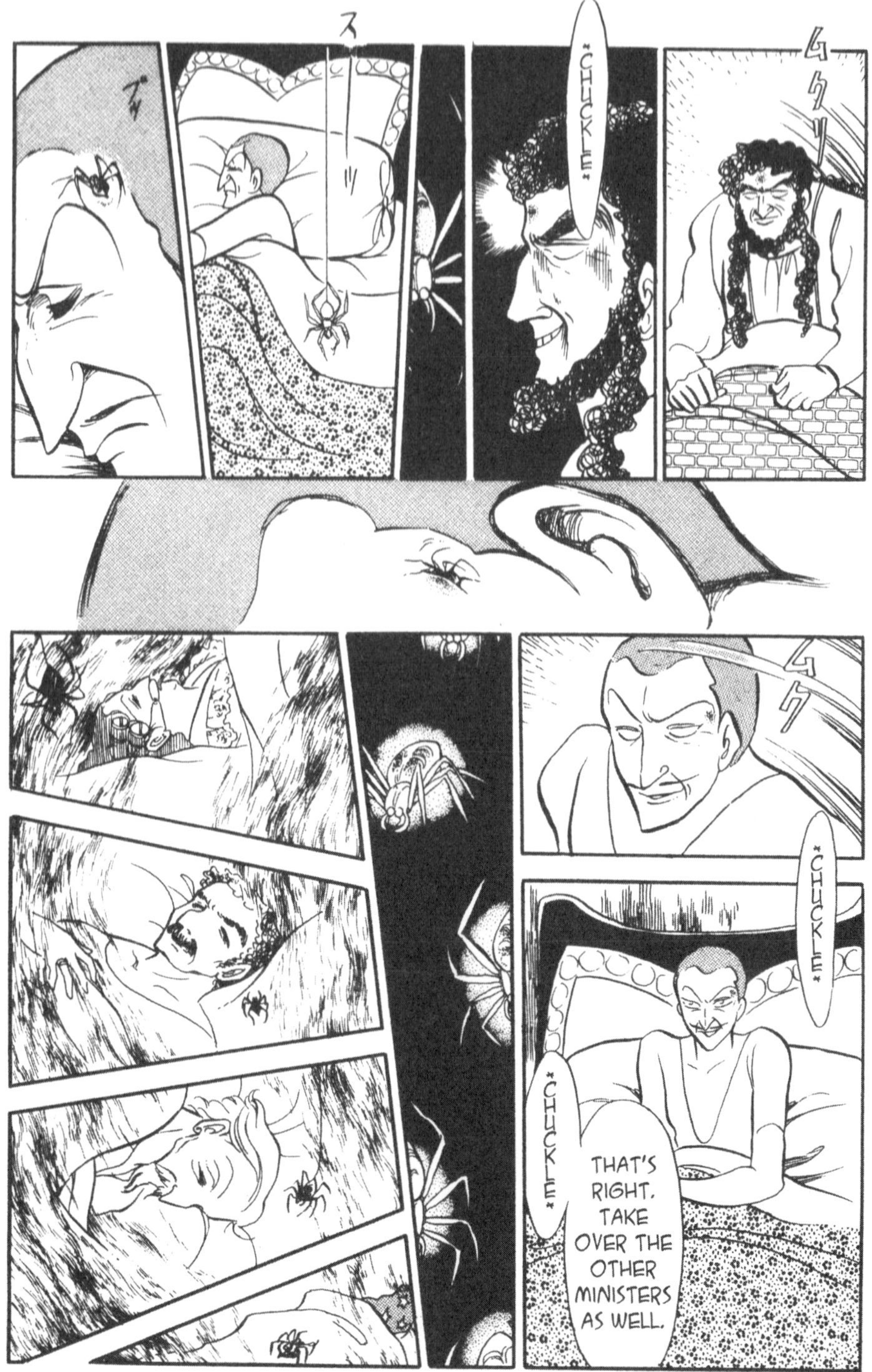
ムクリ
CHUCKLE
ス
ムク
CHUCKLE
CHUCKLE
THAT'S RIGHT. TAKE OVER THE OTHER MINISTERS AS WELL.

AAH!
SOMEBODY HELP ME!
SOMETHING EVIL
IS COMING INTO ME...!
SO MANY EVIL SOULS
IN ONE MIX!
I'M IN PAIN!
KILL ME...
JUST KILL ME!

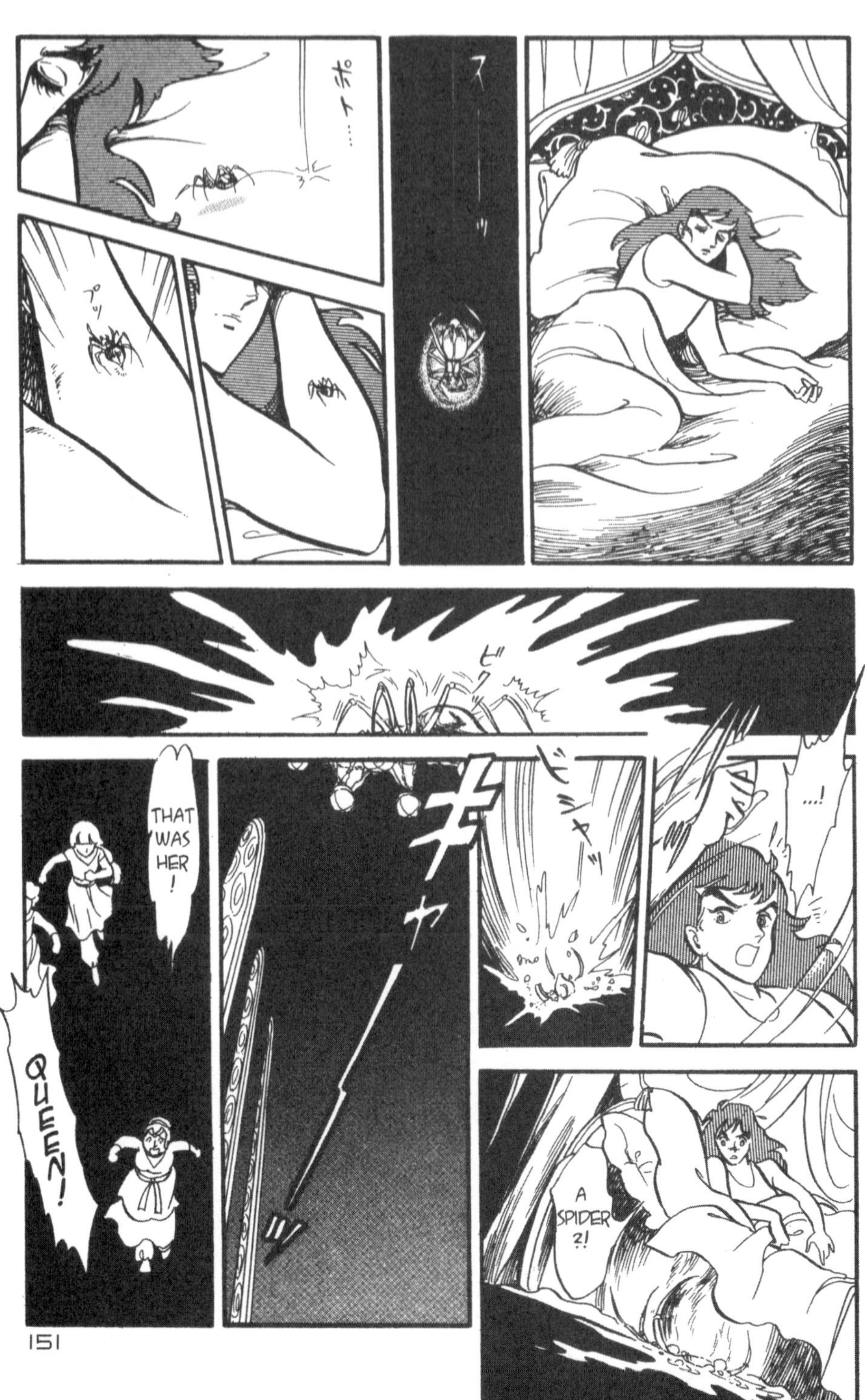
...!
A SPIDER?!
THAT WAS HER!
QUEEN!

A SPIDER TRIED TO... ATTACK ME ...
I-IT'S ALL RIGHT NOW. IT'S DEAD. DEAD!
IT WAS FEARLESS!
UGH, GREEN BLOOD
GET RID OF IT!
BROTHER, GOING BACK SO SOON!
I'M SORRY, LILIA...
I PROMISED FATHER I'D BE BACK IN 5 DAYS TO ASSIST HIM IN STATE AFFAIRS.

DEAR, BELOVED BROTHER
THE ONLY PERSON I TRUST...
WHAT CAN I SAY?
WHAT CAN I SAY TO KEEP YOU HERE?
I'LL RETURN FOR A LONGER VISIT WHEN THE CHILD IS BORN.
YOU'LL BE A MOTHER IN 2 MONTHS. STAY STRONG!
ARE YOU SAD?
HA, SO HE'S GONE.
LILIA, MY DEAR LILIA.
STAY BY MY SIDE!
NO, I AM...

LOOK OUT FOR THE SAND SPOUT!
LOOK! A RED SAND-STORM.
GRAMPS'S SHAKING IN A HOLE.
LEGEND SAYS THE YEAR IT HAILS RED SAND, BAD THINGS HAPPEN.
BAD ...
IT'S A BAD OMEN, BAD...

WHAT'S WITH ALL THESE SANDSTORMS WE'VE BEEN HAVING LATELY?
IN THE MONTH THE CHILD IS TO BE BORN, TOO!
TEE HEE! HOW AWFUL!
WHAT IF SHE GIVES BIRTH TO A DOG?
SNICKER
YOU!
WHAT DID YOU JUST SAY?! LET'S HEAR IT.
HUH?
I... DIDN'T SAY A WORD
WASN'T ME.
...OKAY.
I MAY BE A TAD ON EDGE. NOW GO!

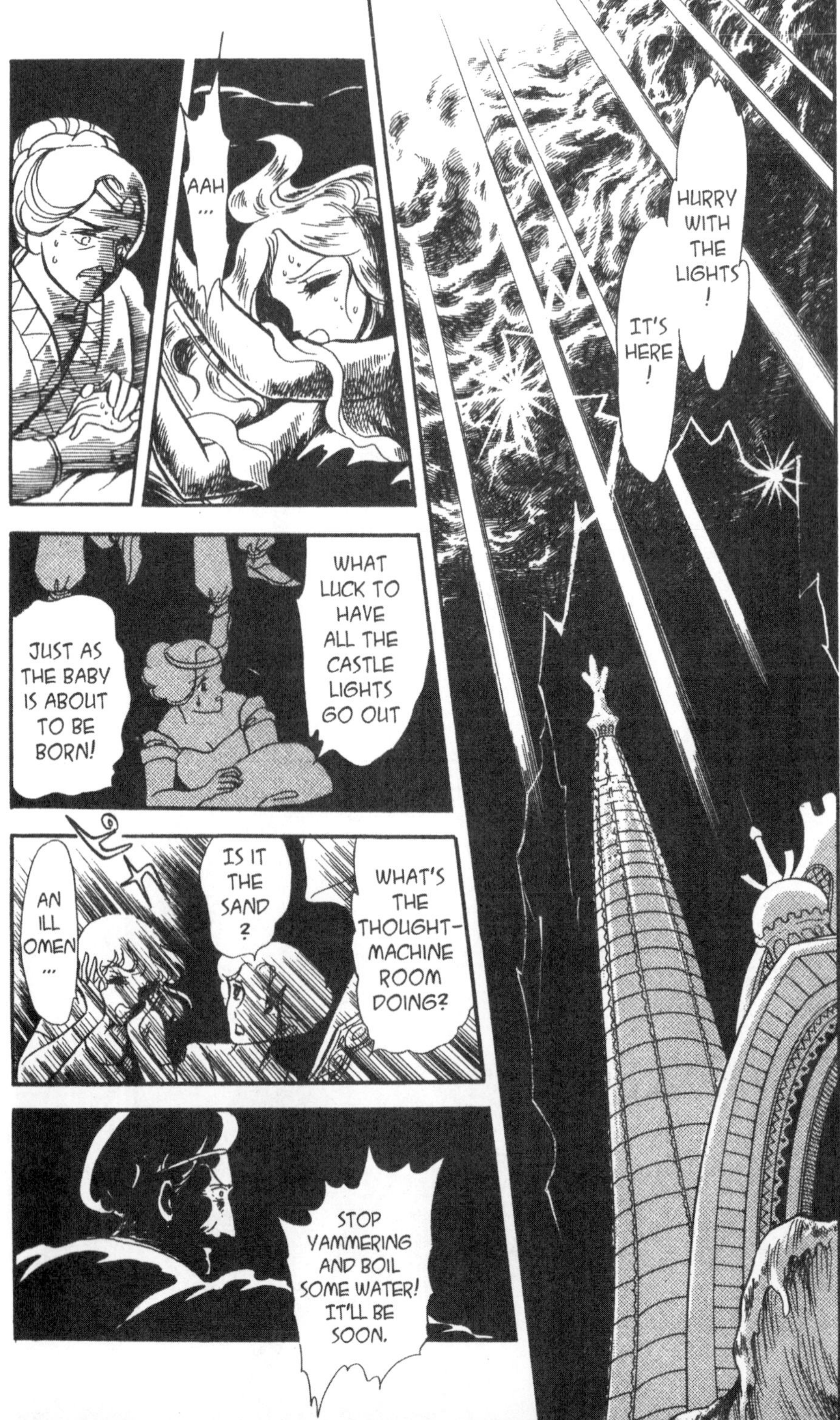
HURRY WITH THE LIGHTS!
IT'S HERE!
AAH...
WHAT LUCK TO HAVE ALL THE CASTLE LIGHTS GO OUT
JUST AS THE BABY IS ABOUT TO BE BORN!
WHAT'S THE THOUGHT-MACHINE ROOM DOING?
IS IT THE SAND?
AN ILL OMEN...
STOP YAMMERING AND BOIL SOME WATER! IT'LL BE SOON.

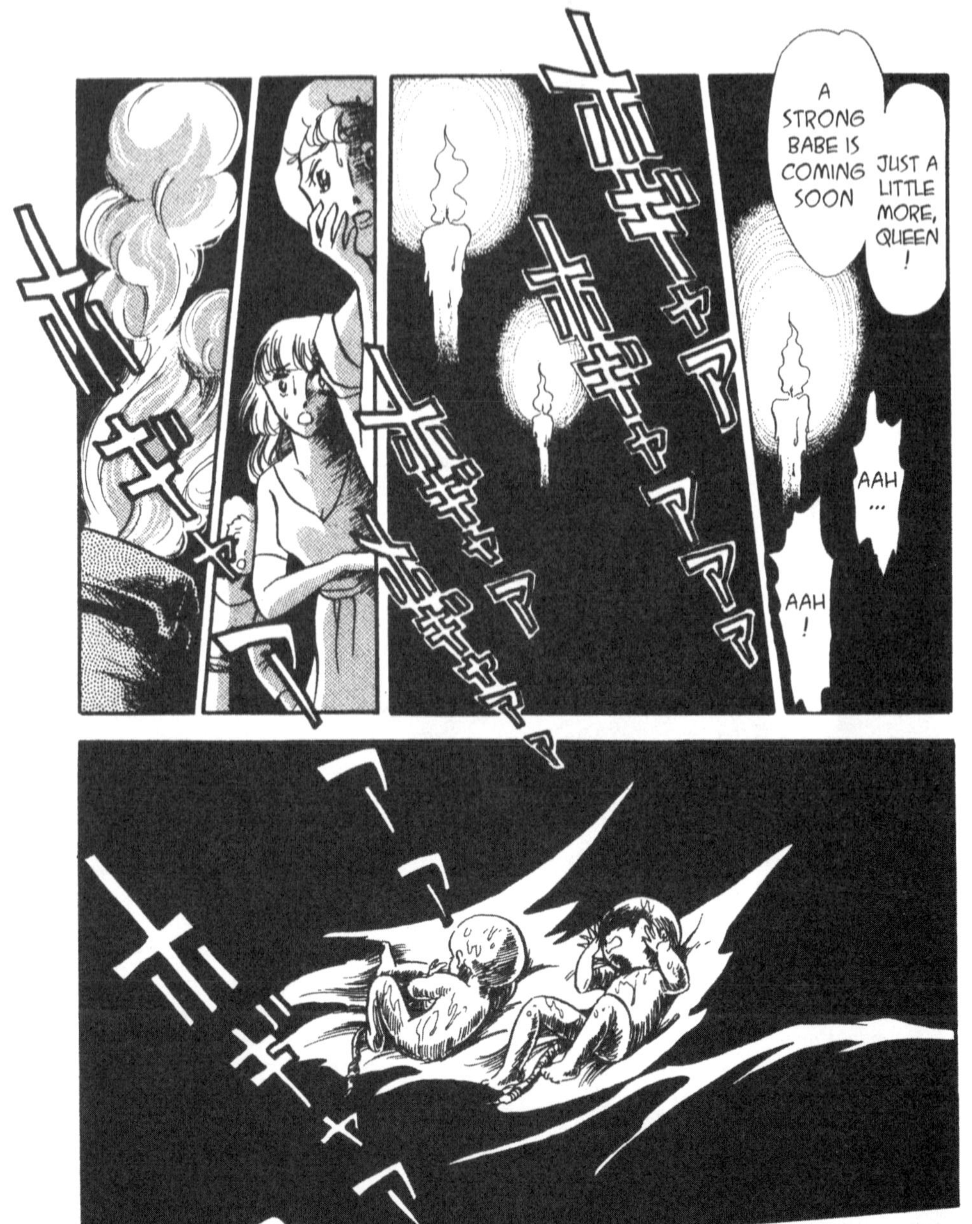
JUST A LITTLE MORE, QUEEN!
A STRONG BABE IS COMING SOON
AAH...
AAH!
THIS IS...

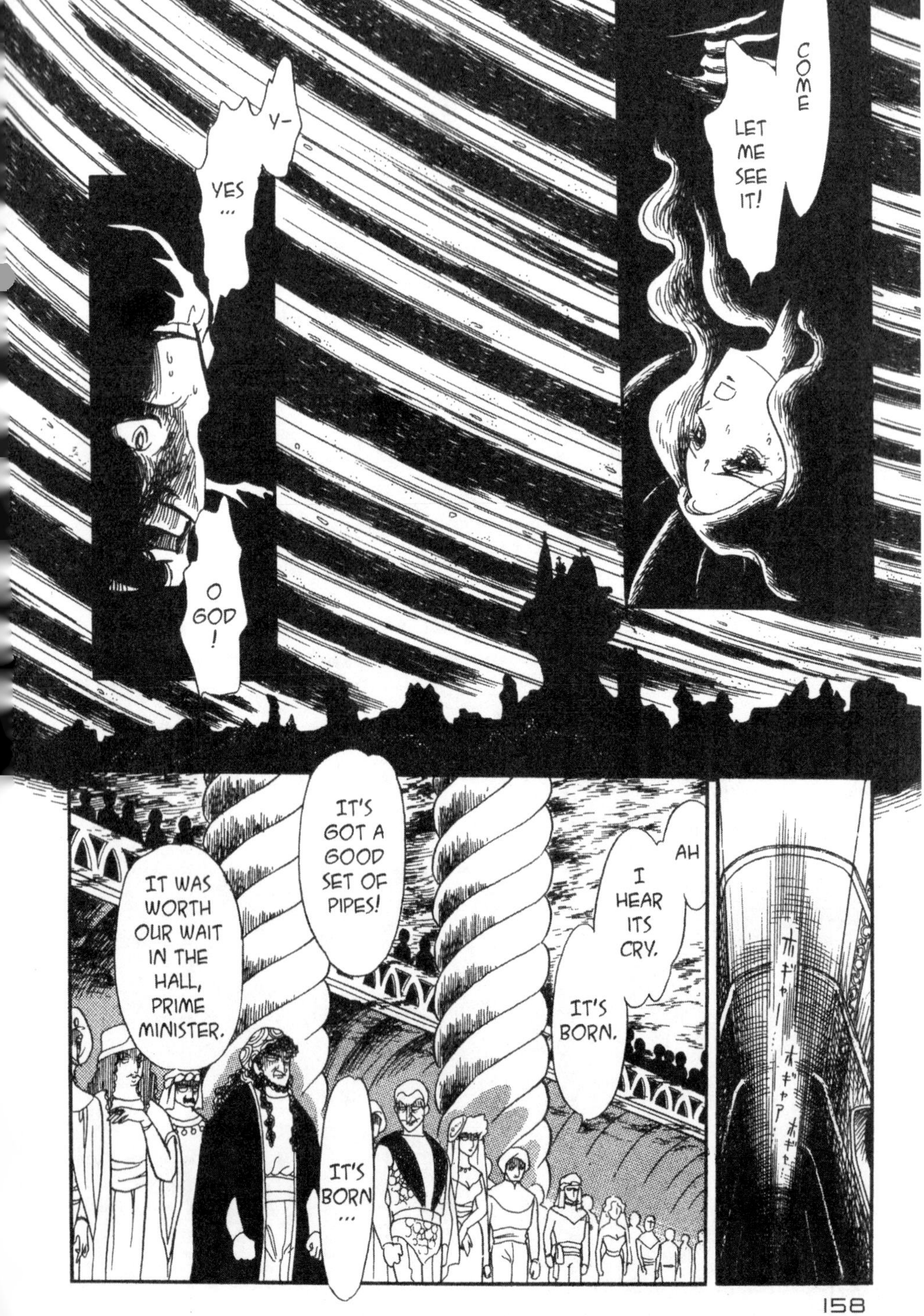

COME
LET ME SEE IT!
Y-
YES...
O GOD!
ホギャー… ホギャア ホギャ…
AH
I HEAR ITS CRY.
IT'S BORN.
IT'S GOT A GOOD SET OF PIPES!
IT WAS WORTH OUR WAIT IN THE HALL, PRIME MINISTER.
IT'S BORN...

THIS IS ...!
HOW COULD THE QUEEN, OF ALL
SILENCE!
THE FATE OF THE REALM HANGS ON THIS.
WHAT ...
IS ANYTHING WRONG WITH MY BABY ?!
A MOMENT PLEASE. WE NEED SOME LIGHT.
TAKE THAT BABY TO HER! IT MATTERS NOT WHICH ...
THE ONE ON THE RIGHT!
ホギャ ホギャア ホギャ
LOOK, QUEEN!
IT'S A PRINCE!
OH
SUCH A DARLING PRINCE!
MY BABY!

DOCTOR! ARE YOU SAYING WE'LL LEAVE IT OUT TO DIE?
IT'S AN AGE-OLD LAW OF THE LAND: TWO HEIRS AT ONCE INVITES CALAMITY...
MORE SO IF THEY ARE HEIRS TO THE KING!
WE MUST AVOID ILL FATE.
HAND ME IT ...
NO...! I-I WILL GET RID OF THIS CHILD.
IT'S STILL THE KING'S.
I'LL TAKE CARE OF IT
THAT CHILD IS NO PRINCE. THERE CAN'T BE TWO!
UGH
FUTILE ...
IN THE END IT MUST DIE...
OOH, SUCH LOUD CRIES! STRONG BABY.

ARGH
BLAST IT, SO I'M NOT CUT OUT FOR BRAINWORK!
THANKS TO THAT THING, I LOST MY CHANCE TO GET BOOZED!
LET'S SEE... THE QUEEN WAS READY TO GIVE BIRTH.
HAS SHE YET?
HM?
WHO STANDS THERE...?
TAKE THIS BABE AND FLEE.
WHAT? BABE?
WHO ARE YOU?!
COME HERE, GLADIATOR!
I SHALL ONLY SAY THIS ONCE.
GLADIATOR, TO WHOM DO YOU PLEDGE FEALTY?
NE'ER YOU MIND!
HIS MAJESTY THE KING!

THEN TAKE THIS CHILD FOR HIS MAJESTY AND LEAVE THIS CITY
AND THIS LAND!
ビクッ
ザ!!
WHAT DO THEY CALL YOU?
BALGA, GREATEST GLADI-ATOR IN THE REALM!
THEN DO THIS.
YES!
DO NOT TELL A SOUL!
!?
I- IS THIS ...?

BABE?
BABE...
WHOSE?
IT WAS JUST BORN....

QUICK, GO!
TO A FAR PLACE NONE SHALL KNOW!

THE QUEEN'S ...?
CAN'T BE!
WHY WOULD IT BE WITH ME?

DEAR GOD!
OHH
MAY THE CHILD GROW SAFE AND SOUND!

YOUR MAJESTY

WE MINISTERS BLESS THE BIRTH OF YOUR SON ...

MAY COSMO-RALIA PROSPER FOREVER ...

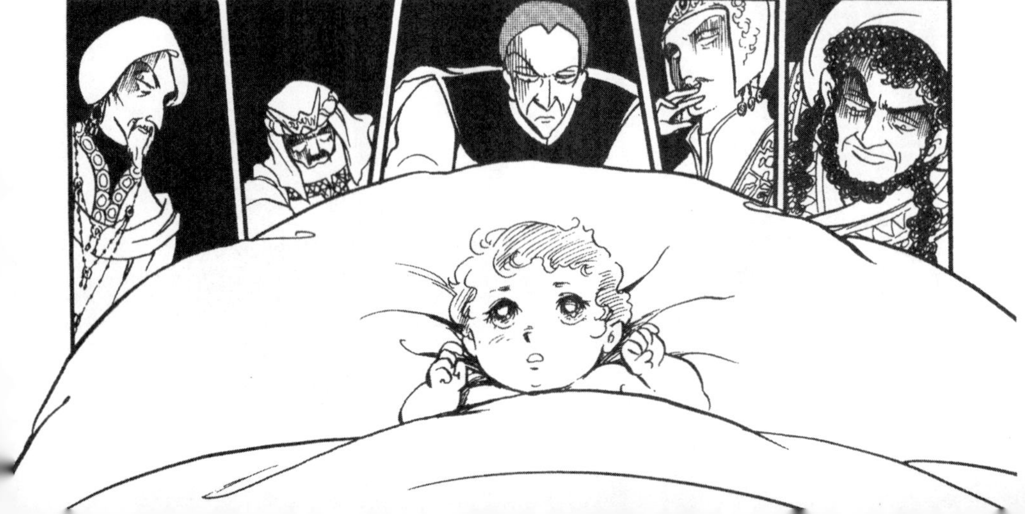

TARAMA! THEY DON'T SEEM STRANGE TO YOU?
IT'S JUST A PASSING FANCY, MY QUEEN.
THEY DO SEEM GLOOMY
WHEN ALL OF COSMORALIA OUGHT TO BE BUBBLING WITH JOY!

WHAT A SPLENDID NAME!
HIS HIGHNESS JIMSA!
HIS HIGHNESS JIMSA...
WHY SO WIDE OPEN, YOUR EYES?
WHAT DO YOU SEEK?
THE QUEEN HAS NOT NOTICED
BUT HE HAS NOT CRIED OR SLEPT FOR A DAY.
IS HE WORRIED ABOUT THE WHEREABOUTS OF HIS OTHER HALF?

HALT ...!
YOU CAN'T EXIT OR ENTER TOWN WITHOUT A PERMIT.
WHAT ?!
WHEN DID THEY MAKE SUCH A RULE ?
THIS WAS A FREE TOWN. WE'RE NOT AT WAR, ARE WE? STOP JOKING AROUND!
JOKING ? WHAT IS THAT ?
PERMIT
REQUIRED!
UH-OH.
...!!
THERE'S NO REASONING WITH THEM.
ARE THEY HUMAN?!

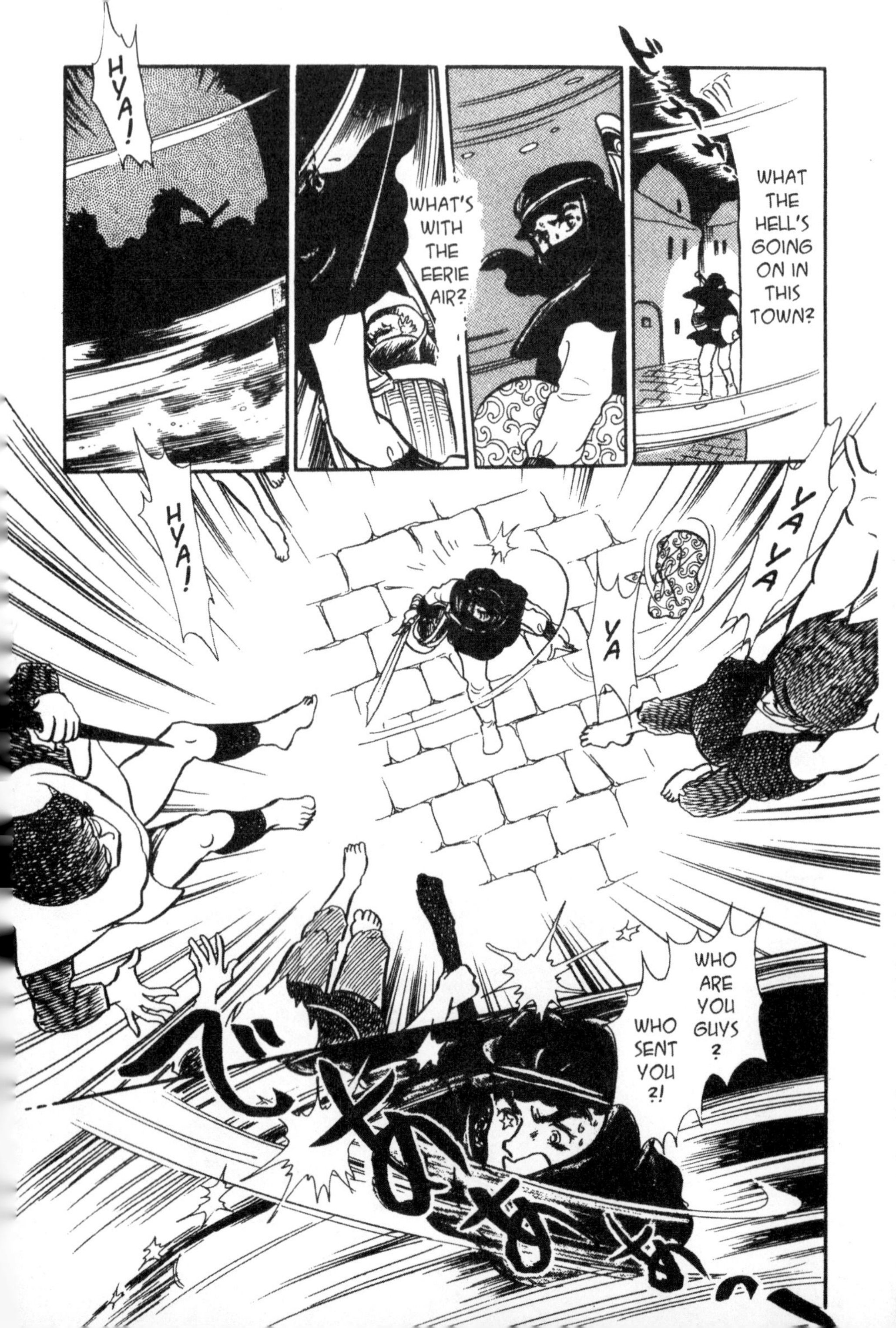
WHAT THE HELL'S GOING ON IN THIS TOWN?
WHAT'S WITH THE EERIE AIR?
HYA!
YA YA YA
YA
HYA!
WHO ARE YOU GUYS?
WHO SENT YOU?!

THE BABY'S GONE!!
HEY!
これこそ
OOPS...
I SHOULD HAVE SPARED ONE TO FIND OUT WHO SENT THEM.
SERVES YOU RIGHT, SUCKERS!
WHAT?!
OVER HERE...
SIR BALGA!
THE WHOLE TOWN'S GOING TO PITS.
THE GUYS WHO JUMPED YOU WERE JUST COMMON THIEVES.
HERE IS YOUR LOST ITEM
COME IN, QUICK!

AWW ... HOW LONG HAS IT GONE UNFED?
IT'S TOO WEAK TO CRY!
WHO ARE YOU?
I'M JUST A GHETTO HOOKER. CORINO'S THE NAME. FAVOR ME.
WHY DO YOU KNOW MY NAME?!
YOU FANCY ...
THERE'S ANYONE WHO DOESN'T, TOP GLADIATOR BALGA?
SIR BALGA, WITH AN INFANT. WHERE TO?
WHATEVER FOR, YOU STAND OUT TOO MUCH.
ほほ...
WHAT COULD I DO?
WHAT A CUTE LITTLE HAND ...
AND SUCH A FIRM GRIP!
ぶぜん
OH...
WHAT'S WRONG? IS IT HURT?
LOOK AT THE BABY'S PALM!!

A RED DRAGON CREST ...!
HUH?
DOES THAT BIRTH-MARK MEAN SOME-THING?
WELL, THERE'S THIS LEGEND.
"FROM HEAVEN THE RED DRAGON SEAL DESCENDS—WHEN DREAMS SHATTER AND EMPIRE CRUMBLES, WITH DRAGON WING HE SHALL BRUSH AWAY EVIL. A DRAGON HOLDS HE."
MEANING, THE SAVIOR OF THE REALM WILL HAVE A RED DRAGON ON HIS PALM.
NO WAY!
ARE YOU SAYING THIS IS THAT PRINCE?
PRINCE?! THIS BABY ...?
NO! NO... THEY WOULDN'T HAND ME... THE NEWBORN PRINCE...
HEAR!
HE IS BORN!
A PRINCE IS BORN!

DEAR GOD!
THEN THE QUEEN GAVE BIRTH TO "DOUBLE HEIRS"?
...
MY STAR!
I'VE FINALLY FOUND IT...
FOR YEARS AND YEARS I'VE WAITED...
HEY...
SEEING MEN FOR MONEY...
I'D HALF GIVEN UP...
WOMAN! SAY A WORD OF THIS AND YOU'RE DONE FOR!
I CAN FINISH YOU NOW
ふん
HA!
AND HOW WILL YOU HIDE THAT FRAME OF YOURS?
...!
HOW WILL YOU GET OUT OF TOWN?
UM...

ME, I COULD PASS US OFF FOR MOTHER AND CHILD
AND EVEN NURSE HIM!

COME TO ME... MY CHILD!

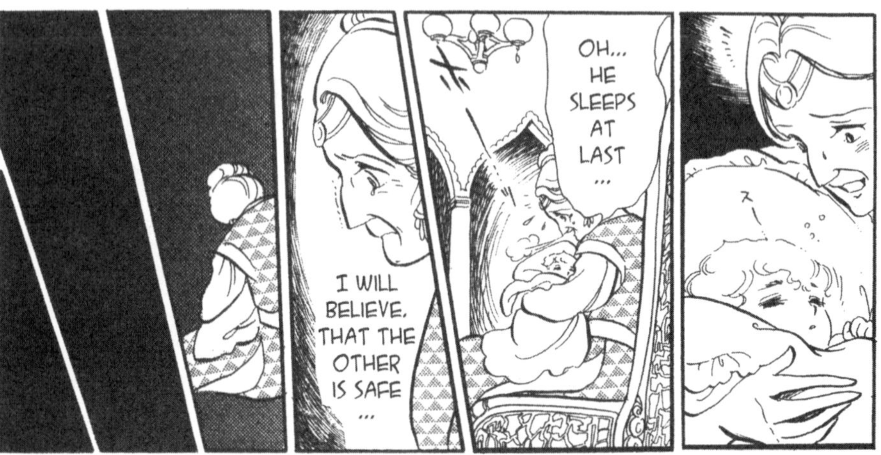
OH... HE SLEEPS AT LAST...
I WILL BELIEVE. THAT THE OTHER IS SAFE...

WHY, MY LORD?
WHAT NEED IS THERE TO REMAKE THE CITY?
I HEAR THAT THE PEOPLE HAVE BEEN DRIVEN FROM THEIR ABODES, OUT INTO THE COLD!
HAVE THE KING AND HIS MINISTERS NO EAR LEFT FOR THEM?
WHY SHOULD YOU BE SO HARSH, MY LORD?

SHUT UP!
YOU WILL NOT DEFY ME!
IT IS TO HONOR THE BIRTH OF CROWN PRINCE JIMSA!
S-STOP, KING! RAISING YOUR HAND AGAINST YOUR QUEEN!!
HMPH!
LOWLIFE DESERVE NO PITY!
KING! FROM AYODOYA THE PRINCE COMES.
BEWARE...
CHASE HIM AWAY,
OR BETTER, TAKE HIS LIFE!
ニヤ
AAH!

AAAH!
AAH?
AAH!
AAH
OH, JIMSA ...
YOU WOULD CONSOLE ME?
AAA?
...!

おいおいおい
OH, TARAMA... IT'S OKAY...
I CAN CARRY ON
AS LONG AS JIMSA IS WITH ME!
SEE, I'M ABLE TO
LAUGH...
THE KING MUST BE ILL. FROM OVERWORK.
WHY ELSE SHOULD A MAN AS KIND AS PRINCE ITHACA
CHANGE SO MUCH?
OH, TARAMA...
HOW CAN I PUT HIM IN GOOD SPIRITS?
MAYBE IF I WEAVE AGAIN...
OR...
PRINCESS!
SHAME ON ME!!
I'M OF SO LITTLE HELP...

AH, SO IT WAS YOUR CONVOY, AYODOYAN PRINCE!
ARCHDUKE RILIÉTE. DO YOU RIDE TO MEET THE NEWBORN TOO?
AAH, RIGHT, THE BRIDE OF ASTRALTA III IS YOUR...
SISTER, YES...
THE POOR QUEEN ...
...THE KING IS LIKE A DIFFERENT MAN...
SHH!

THE ONCE BEAUTIFUL ARAN-CHAN!
TODAY IT BRISTLES WITH STRANGE BUILDINGS.
THEIR PEOPLE HAVE GONE BAD... THEIR BORDER TOWNS ARE THIEVES' DENS.
THE DESERT SPREADS. ONLY A FEW OASES REMAIN ...
SAY A WORD AGAINST THE CROWN AND
THE SECRET POLICE WHISKS YOU AWAY!!
A DARK REIGN!
NOT JUST THE KING. HIS MINISTERS HAVE ALSO GONE MAD...
NAY, THE PEOPLE TOO, IF ONLY LESS SO ...
EVEN THE WEATHER IS OUT OF JOINT ...
AND IT SEEMS THE NEW NORM.

OHH...
IS THAT THE SAME ARANCHAN WE SAW NOT LONG AGO?!
WHAT ARE THOSE TOWERS?
TANKS GUARD THE CITY WALLS!

THIS ...

IS THE FRUIT OF AN ENTIRELY DIFFERENT CIVILIZATION.
EASY...

HALT!
PASSING THROUGH THE GATES WITHOUT A VALID REASON IS FORBIDDEN.

A STRANGE
MECHANICAL VOICE!
I AM MILAN OF AYODOYA KINGDOM
HERE TO SEE YOUR QUEEN.

PRINCE MILAN MAY PASS ...

YOU MAY PASS!
...

HURRY IT UP, YOU SLOTHS !!
F-FOR THE KING!
LONG LIVE THE KING !!

THIS TIME, LILIA, I COME TO TAKE YOU AWAY FROM THIS COUNTRY.
I CAN'T LEAVE YOU IN SUCH A PLACE.
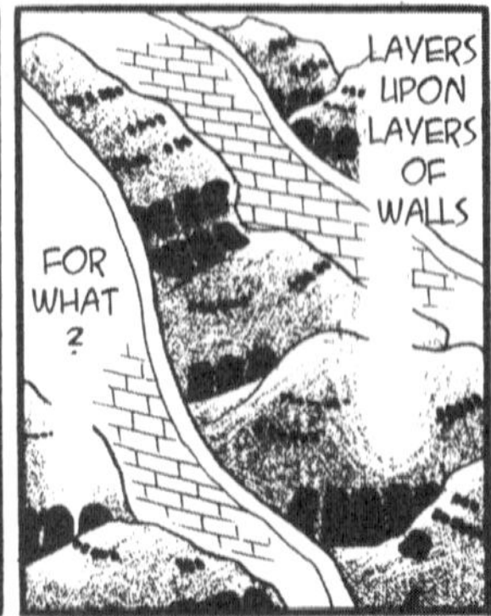
LAYERS UPON LAYERS OF WALLS
FOR WHAT?

THE SAND SMELLS FUNNY.
NO WONDER THEY'VE GONE MAD, LIVING AMIDST THIS SAND.

THE AGENTS I SENT TOLD ME THINGS WERE BAD,
BUT THIS ...

ヘヘヘヘ
ケラケラケラ
AH, YOUR MAJESTY!
WE WERE ON OUR WAY TO GREET YOU, HOLY KING.
...
WHO ARE YOU?
I AM GODAI, OF A LONG LINEAGE OF GLADIATORS SERVING THIS REALM.
THIS HERE IS MY SON BALGA, WHO'LL BE SERVING AS BODYGUARD TO THE CROWN PRINCE.
OW

LIFT YOUR FACE
BUT NOT YOUR HEAD!
HIS EYES!
DID THEY JUST CLICK?
HEY, GET UP NOW,
YOU DUMB OAF! A BIG BABY AREN'CHA?
CHILL. THIS NUMBSKULL IS TRYING TO FIGURE THINGS OUT, TOO.
A ROBOT? NAH...
DON'T TAX YOUR BRAIN, SLOWPOKE!
MAYBE LIKE THAT SPIDER—MADE TO LOOK REAL?
OOPS!!
OUCH!!

IT'S THE QUEEN'S NURSE! PLEASE FORGIVE MY SON!
?
?
?
シカジカ
コレコレ
IS THAT SO?
THE PRINCE'S BODY-GUARD? VERY WELL, COME THIS WAY...
HE NEEDS TO GET DRESSED HERE.
SEE YA, POPS!
!
OH... OKAY.

COME IN ...
THIS IS MY ROOM. WE'RE ALONE.
... SO YOU ARE THAT LADY FROM ...
WHAT KIND OF MAN ARE YOU ?!
I IMPLORED YOU TO CARE FOR THAT CHILD. WHAT DID YOU DO WITH IT?!
WELL, WHAT DID YOU DO WITH IT? FINE WORDS COMING FROM A HEARTLESS WOMAN!
I DON'T CARE IF THERE WAS A REASON. A MOTHER'S STILL GOT TO RAISE HER KID!!
I TOOK ON COURT DUTY TO TELL THE QUEEN MYSELF!
OH!

AND SO... WHERE IS THE CHILD?
SHE BEARS NO GUILT. SHE STILL DOES NOT KNOW.
グスン
UM, I'D RATHER THE QUEEN CRIED IN MY ARMS...
さめざめ
ドカッ!
ALL I KNOW IS THAT THE WOMAN WHO FLEW WITH THE PRINCE SAFELY EXITED THE CITY.
THERE'S NO TELLING WHERE SHE WENT AFTERWARDS.
MY APOLOGIES! I'VE HAD NEARBY REALMS SEARCHED TOO, BUT THERE IS NO CLUE.
THERE'S NO NEWS OF THEIR DYING, EITHER.
THEN... PERHAPS THEY'RE LIVING HAPPILY TOGETHER SOMEWHERE...
MAYBE IT WAS FOR THE BEST.
IF HE WERE PRINCE, HE'D BE IN DANGER.
NURSE!
I'M SORRY FOR HITTING YOU EARLIER.
THANKS TO YOU, I'VE REGAINED MYSELF.
YEAH, SORRY TO HIT YOU BACK...

?
MUM?
AHH?
GUEST COME!
OH!
DID YOU JUST SPEAK, PRINCE JIMSA? SAY IT AGAIN!
GUEST COME
YA?
HE COME SOON,
MUM'S ALLY...
IT'S ONLY BEEN FOUR MONTHS (EIGHT EARTH MONTHS), AND YOU'RE SUDDENLY TALKING...
PRINCE JIMSA!
YOU'VE FORETOLD BROTHER'S ARRIVAL!
MY QUEEN! I HAVE NEWS!
HIS HIGHNESS PRINCE MILAN HAS JUST ARRIVED FROM AYODOYA TO CONGRATULATE YOU.

IT'S GOOD TO SEE YOU WELL,
ASTRALTA III!
I'VE COME TO OFFER WORDS OF BLESSING AND TO CALL ON THE QUEEN.

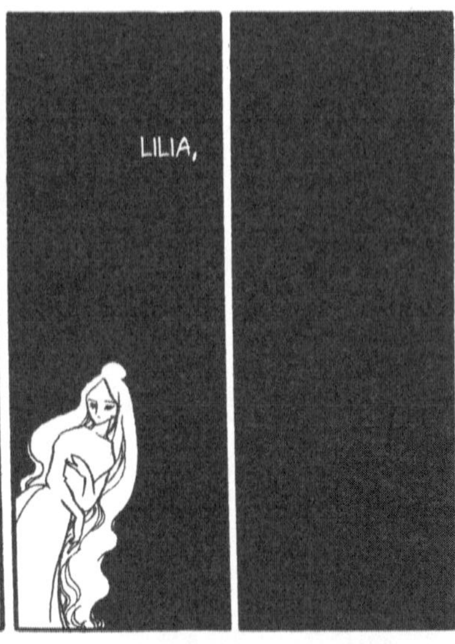

EVEN YOUR BELOVED KING

IS UNDER A BOND!

WELCOME!
I AM MILAN, HERE TO SEE QUEEN LILIA.
...
KING
DO YOU SEE?
THE RUSE OF THOSE WHO'D BETRAY YOU...
HATE THEM. YOU MUST KILL THEM NEXT.

KING, GO FORTH
ALL'S READY. CAPTURE THEM, AND
KILL THEM!

YOU MUST COME HOME WITH ME!

IF I COULD, I'D ASK THE KING TO COME AS WELL.

LILIA, OUR ELDERLY FATHER IS WORRIED, TOO. TELL THEM YOU NEED SOME REST.

NO, I'M NOT COMING!

YOU CAN'T ASK THAT OF THE PRINCESS ...

PRINCE MILAN, YOU'VE JUST ARRIVED!

LILIA, ARE YOU AWARE OF WHAT'S GOING ON? WHAT BEAUTIFUL ARANCHAN NOW LOOKS LIKE?

NO!

BUT IF THERE IS SOMETHING, THEN I MUST STAY BY HIS MAJESTY'S SIDE.

I AM HIS BRIDE

AND PRINCE JIMSA'S MOTHER ...

EVEN SO, DOES ASTRALTA III CARE FOR YOU AS MUCH?
!
LILIA!
I AM TAKING YOU BACK HOME NO MATTER WHAT!
I HAVE VOWED TO DO SO!
LILIA!
SHH...

VERY WELL.

DID HE CATCH ON?
WILL I HAVE ANOTHER CHANCE TO SEE LILIA?

PRINCE MILAN! COME BACK SOON!

DID THAT CHILD SAY IT?!
HE HARDLY MOVED HIS MOUTH!

A VINE CONNECTS THE HALL BALCONY TO THAT WINDOW.
USE IT TO GET BACK.

ガヤガヤ
ワイワイ
WHAT A SIGHT! THIS COUNTRY'S LONG—
WE NEED TO ESCAPE... FAST.
I— I NEED SOME FRESH AIR.
WHERE ARE YOU GOING?

A VINE!
ARGH!

LILIA, WE NEED TO LEAVE HERE NOW! GRAB PRINCE JIMSA!
WHAT ?!
BROTHER!!
I DON'T BELIEVE YOU!!
THEY'RE NO LONGER HUMAN... ASTRALTA III IS NO MORE!
I DON'T CARE IF YOU DO. WE NEED TO LEAVE NOW. OTHERWISE...
HUH ?!
THIS WAY!
THEY'VE BLOCKED THIS DOOR. IS THERE ANOTHER ?
NO GOOD !!

AN INVISIBLE WALL!
IT'S... CLOSING IN!
TRUE NATURE ?! WHAT ARE YOU...
AT LAST YOU SHOW YOUR TRUE NATURE.
IS ANYONE, ANYONE HERE?
WHERE ARE THE MAIDS?
IT'S NO USE,
LILIA, THIS CASTLE HAS FALLEN INTO ENEMY HANDS!
...
HELP COME.
THERE'S SOMEONE AT THE ENTRANCE!

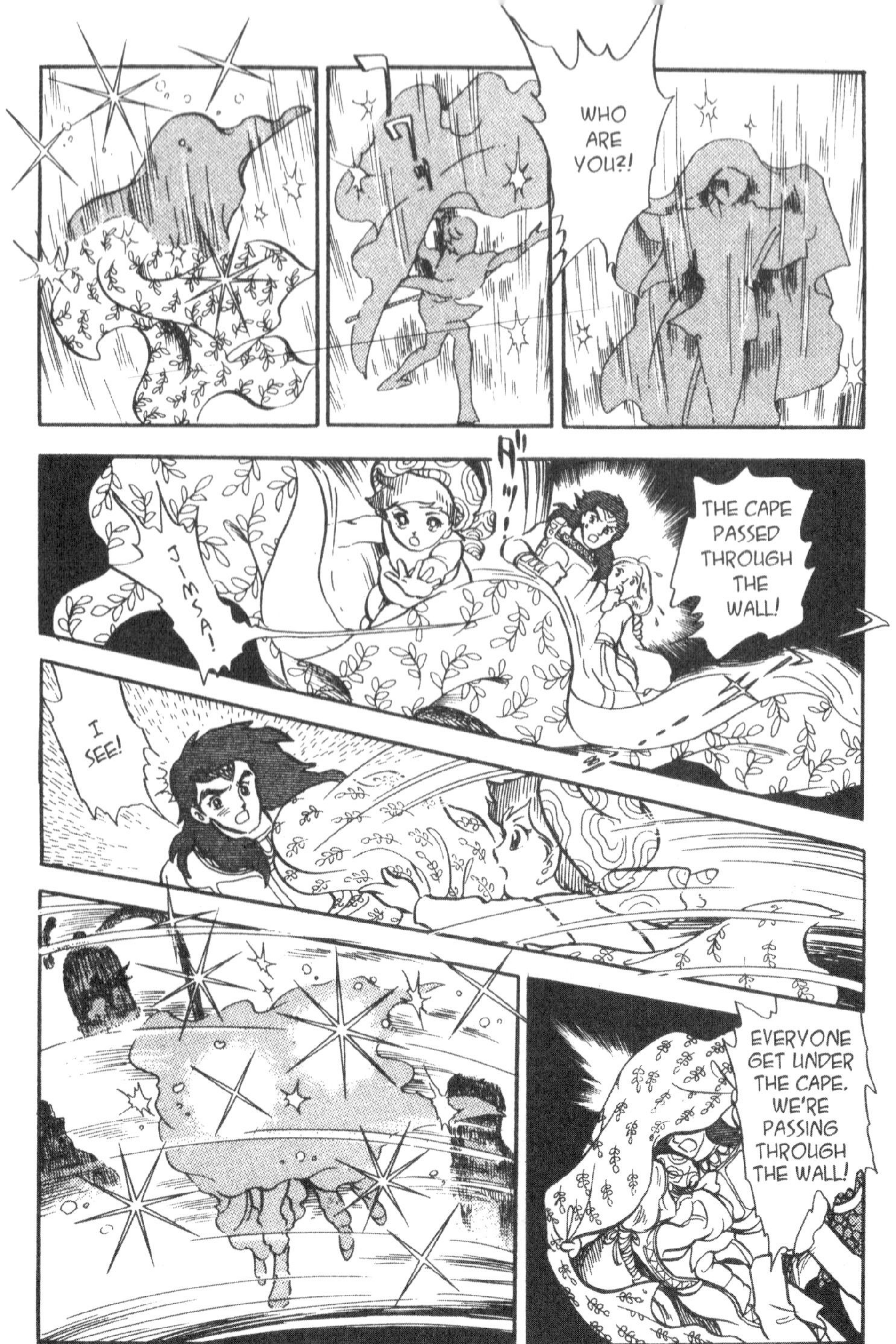
WHO ARE YOU?!
THE CAPE PASSED THROUGH THE WALL!
JIMSA!
I SEE!
EVERYONE GET UNDER THE CAPE, WE'RE PASSING THROUGH THE WALL!

HURRY, THIS WAY! A HIDDEN STAIRCASE LEADS OUT OF HERE.
BUT WHO ARE YOU ?

GOOD THING I WAS NEAR, SEARCHING THE CASTLE.
COME!

MY NAME IS IL. FOR NOW, DON'T ASK MORE. I'M YOUR ALLY, OR RATHER ...
THEIR ENEMY

THEY HAVE FOUND HIDDEN STAIR-CASE D-14.
TURN ON THE FIRE SPRAY!

THE CITY'S DONE FOR.
SO MANY MADMEN. THEY WREAK HAVOC...
TERRIBLE
IT MUST BE DUE TO THE SANDSTORMS. THE WINDS NEVER DIE DOWN. SAND INVADES THE CITY.
LUCKILY OUR COMRADES, THEIR SPOUSES AND CHILDREN HAVE NOT BEEN AFFECT-ED...

YOU'RE BORED, BUT NOT AWARE OF WHAT'S GOING ON.
YOU WON'T BE FOR LONG.
TELL ALL WHO ARE HERE WHAT YOU SAW!

UH...

ER... UM...
I...
DON'T THINK THAT KING IS HUMAN.
JUST LIKE THOSE LIFE-LIKE SPIDERS THEY MAKE AT THAT FACTORY,
I BET HE'S SOME ARTIFICE.
WHAT ?!
HOW DARE YOU! YOU'VE PLEDGED FEALTY TO HIM,
THE KING !!
STOP IT!
I FEAR HE SPEAKS THE TRUTH.
THEY ARE SHOWING THEIR TRUE NATURE AT LAST.

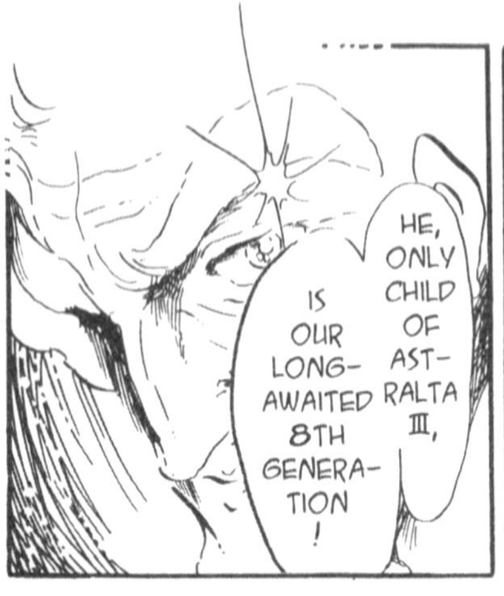
HE, ONLY CHILD OF AST-RALTA III,
IS OUR LONG-AWAITED 8TH GENERA-TION!

FOR...

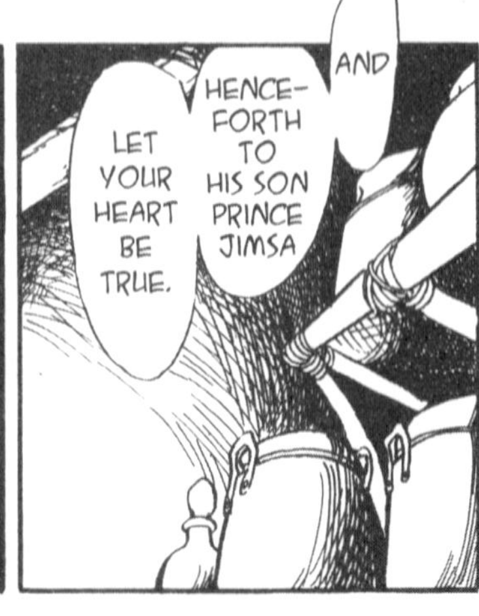
LET YOUR HEART BE TRUE.
HENCE-FORTH TO HIS SON PRINCE JIMSA
AND

THE EIGHTH GENERATION!!

SO PRINCE JIMSA MARKS THE 8TH GENERA-TION!
LONG LIVE THE
PRINCE!!
THEN WE MUST BE EVEN MORE LOYAL TO HIM THAN TO PAST KINGS...

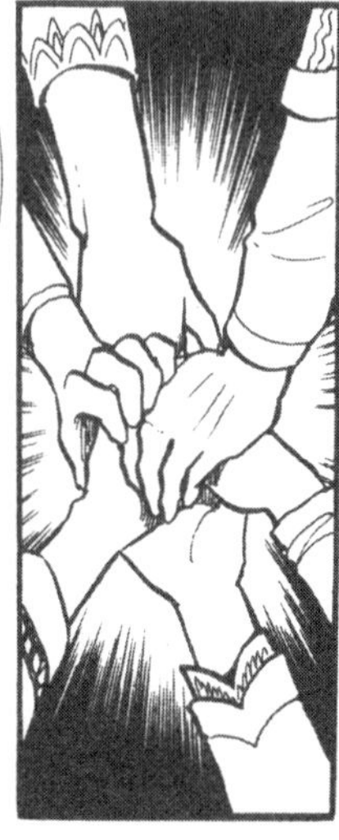

AT LAST!
AHH
LONG WAS OUR WAIT!!

END OF VOLUME 1

TO BE CONTINUED

IN VOLUME 2

ABOUT THE AUTHORS

Keiko Takemiya made her debut in 1968 with "The Sin of the Apple." She is one of a handful of women artists called the 49ers who created shojo manga as we know it today. Takemiya won the 25th Shogakkan Manga Award in 1980 for *To Terra...* and *The Poem of the Wind and the Tree*. In 2000, she became Japan's first-ever "Professor of Manga" at Kyoto Seika University, where she continues to teach. In addition to her own comics, she has penned illustrations for various novels.

Ryu Mitsuse (1928-99) is best known for his science fiction works but also excelled as a writer of historical fiction. He received the Japan SF Award, Special Prize, posthumously. *Ten Billion Noons and a Hundred Billion Nights*, his most popular novel, formed the basis of the celebrated manga by Moto Hagio, Takemiya's fellow 49er. Mitsuse devised an original story for his collaboration with Takemiya on *Andromeda Stories*. He was a major formative influence on Takemiya by her own account.

IN SPACE, NO ONE CAN HEAR YOU CRY

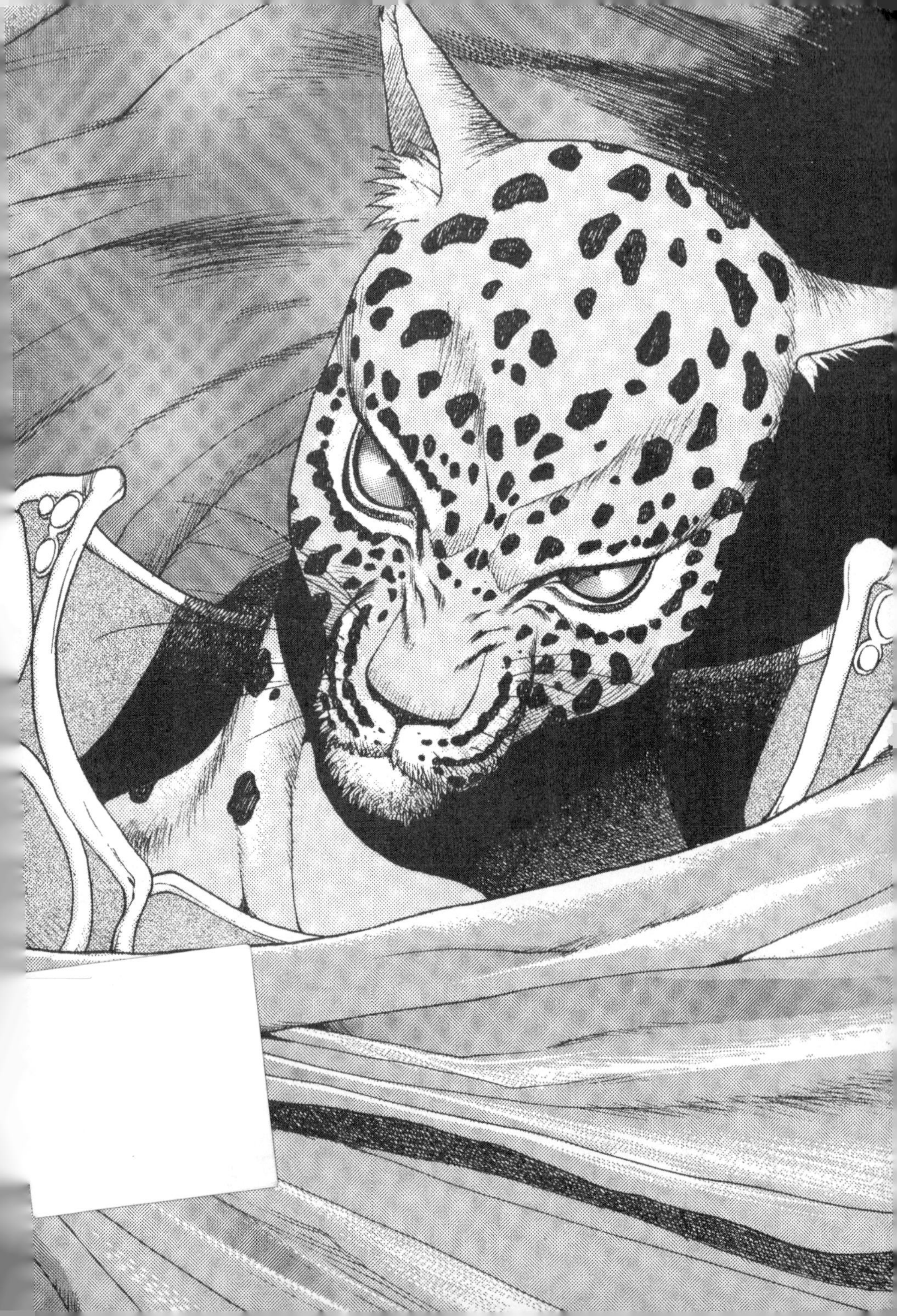

WRONG WAY!

Japanese books, including manga like this one, are meant to be read from right to left.

So the front cover is actually the back cover, and vice-versa.

To read this book, please flip it over and start in the top right-hand corner. Read the panels, and the bubbles in the panels, from right to left, then drop down to the next row and repeat.

It may make you dizzy at first, but forcing your brain to do things backwards makes you smarter in the long run. We swear.